THERE'S NO PLACE LIKE HOME

BOOKS BY WILLOW ROSE

Emma Frost Mysteries

Itsy Bitsy Spider

Miss Polly Had a Dolly

Run, Run, as Fast as You Can

Cross Your Heart and Hope to Die

Peek a Boo, I See You

Tweedledum and Tweedledee

Easy as One, Two, Three

Needles and Pins

Where the Wild Roses Grow

Waltzing Matilda

Drip Drop Dead

Black Frost

Detective Billie Ann Wilde series

Don't Let Her Go

Then She's Gone

In Her Grave

THERE'S NO PLACE LIKE HOME

WILLOW ROSE

bookouture

Published by Bookouture in 2024

An imprint of Storyfire Ltd.
Carmelite House
50 Victoria Embankment
London EC4Y 0DZ

www.bookouture.com

First published by Buoy Media LLC in 2014.

ISBN: 978-1-83525-335-9
eBook ISBN: 978-1-83525-334-2

CONTENT NOTE

This book features graphic scenes of violence. If this is potentially sensitive to you, please read with care.

PROLOGUE

MAY 2014

"What's the worst thing that can happen?"

Jonas looked at Maria with anticipation. She loved his deep blue eyes and curly brown hair. Oh, how she loved him. But she had her doubts. It was a big decision they were about to make. They had just gotten married, and the wedding was expensive. Where they ready to take this step? Could they afford it? Jonas was a dreamer, and not always the most realistic when it came to money. Neither was she.

"Think about it," Jonas continued. "I know we're in a little over our heads with this one financially, but it's the house we've dreamt of. It's the one we want. None of the others made us excited like this one does. And it's right on the beach. What's not to love?"

He grabbed the listing from the table and went through the pictures once again. Maria felt a strange sensation in her body. She wasn't sure exactly what it was. She loved the house. No doubt about it. But, was it too soon? Would it be too hard for them financially? Was it the best choice? It was, by far, the most expensive of the houses they had been looking at. She couldn't put her finger on it, but something inside her told her they shouldn't do it.

She looked at the pictures over Jonas's shoulder.

But it's perfect. It's beautiful. It's all I've ever dreamt of.

"It might be hard in the beginning," Jonas said. "Maybe the first couple of years, but I'm soon up for that promotion. I mean, they've got to give it to me after all the work I put in on that last case."

"You did work hard on that one. And you did win it," Maria said.

"I know. They have to promote me. I'm next in line, the way I see it, and Juhlsen even hinted at it the other day when I was in his office."

"He did?"

"Yeah," Jonas paused, and looked with dreaming eyes at the listing. "There is no way they're not giving it to me. No way. And you just got a job at the library as well. I mean, we are going to make good money for the next several years. We can afford this. I really believe we can. It might be tight for a few years, but that's all, the way I see it."

"Really?" Maria said. "You really think we could do it? You think we could buy it?"

She felt a thrill of cold run down her spine. It made her shiver slightly. She was getting more and more excited about this. It was the house of her dreams... more than she could have dared to ever actually dream of. It was the house she could see herself in. Heck, she could even picture herself having kids there.

So, why was she hesitating? Why was she holding back? It was just this strange sense, this feeling, this unsettling emotion inside of her that made her pause.

Jonas clearly didn't have any doubts anymore. "So, what do you say?" he asked, as he took her hand in his and kissed the top of it. "Are you onboard?"

"I... I don't know..." Maria said.

"Come on," Jonas exclaimed. "Why are you being like this?"

"I just... I don't know, Jonas. I just feel like... maybe it's just... I can't escape this feeling that it's a bad idea. That's all."

"A bad idea? How can buying the house of our dreams be a bad idea?" Jonas said with a slightly indulgent smile. He held her hand tightly and looked her in the eyes. "Listen. I know this is a big step for us. I know how difficult big changes are for you. It's perfectly understandable. I'm shaking a little myself. This is a big deal. It really is. But this house is perfect for us. It's screaming for us to move in. Look at this picture. Our new dining room table that we got for our wedding will be perfect on those old wooden floors. Can't you see it?"

Maria swallowed before she looked at the picture. Her heart melted.

She could see it. She really could. She closed her eyes.

"You see it too, don't you?" Jonas asked excitedly.

She nodded. "Yes, yes I see it." She opened her eyes and looked at her handsome husband.

"So, we're doing it?" he asked.

Maria bit her lip, took one last glance at the picture of the house from the outside, and thought she caught a glimpse of a little girl on a swing hanging from the big tree in the front garden. Everything inside of her screamed not to do it, but she didn't listen. Instead, she looked at Jonas with a soft smile.

"Yes," she sighed. "Yes, we're doing it. We're buying the house."

Jonas shrieked happily and kissed her. She closed her eyes and let him hold her in his arms. She tried to imagine them in the house in order to drown out the unsettling thoughts that kept popping up in her mind. It was all just nonsense. It was just her being terrified of change. She had always been like this.

It was silly. Jonas was right. What was the worst thing that could happen?

ONE

MARCH 2009

The first time she saw him was on TV. She had read about him in the newspapers, but on the day the police took him to the courtroom for him to be tried was the first time she saw him.

Like really *saw* him.

Louise Tanggaard was watching the twenty-four-hour news channel while chopping carrots for the stew she was cooking. Actually, she hadn't been paying much attention to what was said in the broadcast, she wasn't even looking at the screen when the reporter started talking, but when he suddenly told the viewers that the accused was now approaching the entrance of the courtroom, Louise was filled with an overwhelming desire to look up. She stopped chopping and stared at the screen in her kitchen that she'd had installed to be able to watch TV while eating with her cats, Lurifax and Lorianne. She had no idea what it was that made her stop and look, or what it was that made her keep watching. There was just something... no it was some*one* who drew her.

He was walking toward the entrance of the old building that was the courtroom in Copenhagen. Next to him, his attorney tried to keep the hordes of reporters and photographers away. Some of them were yelling their questions out toward him, asking him if he had done it, if he had killed them and dismembered the bodies. They received nothing but a smile from the long-haired guy with the dark sunglasses.

What was it about him that made her look? What was it about this guy? Louise felt so drawn to him, even though she knew he was about to stand trial for having murdered his girl-friend and her two sons from another marriage. She grabbed a chair and stared at the screen, while watching the accused, Bjarke Lund, walk past the cameras. When his lawyer opened the door to the courtroom, Bjarke Lund turned to look directly at the cameras. He lifted his handcuffed hands and saluted. At that moment, Louise was convinced that he was saluting her, not the journalists. That he somehow knew she was watching.

And she knew, from that second, that she loved him.

The bodies were never found. Maybe he didn't do it? Maybe he is innocent? No matter what, he must be feeling so lost. So alone.

Louise looked at the screen, as the face of the man she was now convinced she loved disappeared. Lurifax approached her and jumped into her lap. She caressed him gently, while wondering about this guy. She grabbed the newspaper from the dinner table and started flipping the pages. There it was. There he was. Bjarke Lund was now looking at her from a black-and-white picture. Finally, she saw his eyes. He seemed to be looking back at her. The long beard, the ponytail, the leather vest... everything about him signaled bad news, but Louise felt differently. She felt like she understood him, like she knew him.

"You're just misunderstood, aren't you?" she asked, as she let one of her long red nails caress the picture. "You just need the right woman to help you get back on track. You're not such a bad guy. You're nothing like they say you are. I know you're different. You've just never had anyone take care of you. But I could. I could take good care of you."

The case was still being covered on TV, and suddenly, Bjarke Lund appeared in an interview that had taken place many years earlier, when he was accused of having killed his own mother. He was just a teenager at the time. The story had been the same back then. Her body had never been found. In the interview, Bjarke Lund had painted his face green. "Because this is how the world sees me," he stated, when the interviewer asked. "As pure evil, like the Wicked Witch of the West. In your eyes, I am the archetype of human wickedness. I have already been judged. I don't need to stand trial. You have already decided that I did it."

"So, did you do it?" the interviewer asked. "Did you kill your mother?"

"Have they found her body anywhere? Is she even dead?" Bjarke Lund asked.

"So, you didn't do it?"

"Do you think I did it?"

Louise watched, as Bjarke Lund kept avoiding answering the question, and couldn't stop laughing. This guy was smarter than the journalist, and soon the reporter gave up.

Lurifax tried to get her attention by rubbing himself against her. But, for the first time since Lurifax had come to the house on Fanoe island, his mother had no time for him. She pushed him down and turned up the volume of the TV. Just the sound of Bjarke Lund's voice alone made everything melt inside of her. Now he was talking about his childhood, growing up with a dominant mother whose many boyfriends often abused him. Louise nodded all through the interview and knew exactly how he felt. She also knew what he needed.

Killer or not, just like everybody else, this man needed a woman's love and care.

TWO

JULY 2014

The real estate agent was waiting outside the house when they arrived. Maria and Jonas looked at each other and smiled. *There couldn't be a happier couple in the world*, Maria thought, as Jonas parked the car. They got out and walked to the front door.

The real estate agent smiled widely and dangled the key in front of them, holding it between her long fingernails.

This is it, Maria thought, feeling very excited and smiling from ear to ear. *This is really it. I'm officially a homeowner. Married and now with a house. All grown up. If only Mom were alive to see me. She would be so proud. So happy for me. This is all I've ever dreamt of.*

Maria looked at Jonas, then back at the key, still dangling on its chain hanging from the real estate agent's fingers.

"Who wants to do it?" she asked.

Maria drew in a deep breath. Should she be the one to take the keys? Or was that a guy thing? Did the man of the house expect to do it?

Jonas looked at her. "Go ahead," he said. "You be the first."

Maria felt a tickling sensation. "Really?" She kissed her husband and reached out for the key. She grabbed it and felt its weight. It had been almost two months since they'd signed the papers. Her unease hadn't gone away completely, but she felt better about their decision with every day that passed, and as she stood there with the key in her hand, every doubt seemed to have vanished. It was just like Jonas had said. It was just worry and fear of change. Jonas had asked her to trust him, and that much, she could do.

"Go ahead," the real estate agent said. "Enter your new home."

Maria glanced at Jonas one last time before she walked toward the big wooden front door that she had adored since their first visit to the house. She could smell the ocean from behind the house. It was one of those rare warm summer days in Denmark. It would be her first time living on an island, but she had always loved the ocean and knew she would enjoy it.

She put the key in and turned it while holding her breath. Then, she pushed the door open.

The light coming from the other side of the house almost blinded her. The huge windows leading to the garden and the ocean brought in so much sunlight it was startling. She gasped slightly and stepped inside. Jonas was right behind her. She felt his hand on her shoulder.

"Welcome home," he whispered in her ear.

"It's even more beautiful than I remembered," she said, slightly choked.

If only Mother were here. She would have loved it.

The real estate agent entered behind them. "Home sweet home," she chirped, and closed the door behind them.

Jonas kissed Maria on the cheek. Then he walked past her into the living room. "I told you there would be room for your mother's old chair in the corner," he yelled.

She followed him into the living room. He stood in the corner, smiling. "See? We can put it right here. And then the couch over here, and the TV on the wall like this. It's going to be perfect. You see it?"

"I do," Maria said. "It's going to be perfect."

Jonas clapped his hands together. "The lorry will be here in an hour. Time enough for us to empty the car first. Let's get to it."

The real estate agent thanked them and wished them the best of luck in their new home, then she left. All day, Jonas and Maria worked on furnishing their new home. With every chair and every piece of their life that was put into place, Maria felt more and more at home. Especially about noon when some of the neighbors dropped by with a bottle of wine and some home-baked buns to welcome them to the neighborhood. That almost brought her to tears, and she couldn't wait to get to know all of them better.

By the end of the afternoon, they had all their furniture in place, with help from the moving company, and they were alone at last for the first time. Now, it was just the two of them. Two young newlyweds with the beginning of an entire new life in front of them. It was both exciting and a little scary, Maria thought, while standing in the bedroom, surrounded by moun-tains of boxes and bags. She couldn't wait to get all these things into their places and to decorate the house and make it their home. She couldn't wait for them to start an everyday life here. A life where they went off to work in the morning and couldn't wait to get back to their cozy home in the afternoon. She could see herself living a life in this house. She really could. She could see herself having children here; she could see herself growing old here.

Jonas was right. It is perfect for us. Everything about it is just so... perfect.

They unpacked until darkness fell on the house, and they ordered a late-night pizza from a nearby pizzeria. When it arrived, they sat on the carpet in front of the fireplace in the living room and ate out of the box. Their bodies were sore from carrying boxes and moving furniture, and so tired from a long, but joyful, day. Jonas had brought a bottle of champagne that he now opened. He filled their plastic cups.

"A toast," he said, and lifted his glass. "To our new home."

"No place like it," Maria said, and they sipped their champagne.

They sat in silence for a little while, just staring at the high-vaulted living room with the huge windows leading to the garden and the beach. Outside, it was now dark... at least as dark as it got at this time of year, when the northern lights kept the nights bright. It was getting late.

Maria felt tired. Exhausted even. But happier than ever. Jonas leaned over and kissed her neck. She closed her eyes and enjoyed his touch. She loved him so much. So deeply.

"Mmm..."

"I love you so much, Maria. I can't wait for the rest of our life." His hand undid a couple of buttons on her shirt.

"It's a little late," Maria groaned. "And I'm exhausted. Aren't you tired?"

"Mmm..." Jonas continued. He unbuttoned the rest of the buttons on her shirt and pulled one of her breasts out of her bra.

"Jonas. I'm really tired..." She didn't mean it, and he knew it. They still hadn't reached the point in their marriage when they stopped being all over each other. She loved his touches, and she wanted him all the time. Even now, when she was so worn out she could hardly move her body.

She wanted to have sex with him in their new house for the first time. Just not like this. Not on the floor. The bed was set up in the bedroom, and she wanted them to go in there.

Maria opened her eyes to tell him, but as she did, she let out a scream.

Jonas jumped. "What?"

Maria closed her shirt and held a hand against her breasts to cover herself up. "I saw something," she said.

"What?" Jonas asked.

"I don't know. It was out there, in the garden somewhere. Something was moving."

Jonas combed his hair back with his hand. Then he laughed. "It was probably just a cat or a squirrel or something."

"No," Maria said. "It was bigger. It looked like a person."

"You're just being paranoid again," Jonas said. "Who in their right mind would be out in our garden at this time of night? I tell you, it was nothing. Or maybe it was someone. Maybe it was one of the neighbors looking for their dog or cat that has run off or something. This is a safe neighborhood, Maria. You met them today. They were nice people. Nothing strange about them. Heck, they even gave us wine and buns. Besides, this is an island. There's only one way to get here and to leave here. There can't be much crime. Not successful, that is."

"I guess you're right. But there was someone who was murdered down the street from here. An old lady. Two years ago. Right on this street, Jonas."

Jonas sighed, and then looked at her with compassion. She hated that look. It always made her feel like a young child.

"Yes, there was that old story. We talked about it, but the killer was found, remember?"

"It was a police officer, Jonas."

"I know. But he's gone now, right? So, no more worries."

"There has been other stuff the last two years... a lot actually. I read about it the other day."

Jonas leaned over and kissed her lips. "You read too much," he whispered. "Now, let's get to bed. I want to have sex with my wife on the first night in our new house, no matter who is looking at us from outside those windows. Let them look. Who cares?"

Maria chuckled and pushed him lovingly on the shoulder. "Oh, you..." she said. "You never take me seriously, do you?"

"Nah. Not really."

He grabbed her hand and pulled her up from the floor. He held her in his arms. She could feel how strong he was. She loved that about him. He was a real man. Big hands and long arms to wrap around her. He had been working all day on moving boxes and furniture, and not once did he complain that he was tired. He even had the energy to make love to her... even after a day like this.

Maria had grown up alone with her mother, because her dad left when she was just a young child. During her entire childhood, her mother had been constantly afraid... almost paralyzed by fear at times. She'd had her entire life destroyed by this fear... the fear of almost everything she could come up with, it seemed at times. Some days, it could be a fear of burglars entering the house, on other days it was the fear of being attacked by some random stranger in the street or of eating something that could make her sick, of germs entering her body and killing her. It could be almost anything. But especially hard for Maria was her fear of something bad happening to her. It made Maria's teenage years lonely and devastating... never being able to do what the other kids were allowed to. It became so bad in the end that her mother refused to go outside. The doctor called it a social anxiety disorder and agoraphobia, the anxiety of open spaces. But even worse, she forbade Maria to go outside as well, except to go to school or to the supermarket, since she didn't dare to do that on her own. That was when Maria decided she would rather die than end up like her mother.

But it was easier said than done. Every day of Maria's grown-up life she was fighting her own anxiety and, luckily for her, Jonas helped her tremendously. Especially after her mother killed herself two years ago. Jonas had been there, and he had promised he would take care of Maria. He told her she didn't have to be afraid of anything anymore.

Her unease went away as he pulled her toward the bed and undressed her. She closed her eyes and enjoyed the moment. She was so happy she had him. He and his strong arms made her feel so secure. She felt like nothing in this world could ever touch her, could ever touch them.

For the first time in her life, she felt perfectly safe.

THREE

JULY 2014

Jesper Melander looked at the couple having sex in their new home for the first time through the big window leading to the bedroom. He had the best view and enjoyed every moment of it. He knew they wouldn't pull the curtains, because the people from the curtain company weren't coming until the next day to put them up.

He watched as the husband climbed on top of his wife and entered her. He licked his lips and kept watching this delicious scene until the couple were done and fell apart on the bed moaning and breathing hard. It made Jesper Melander even more excited.

Jesper Melander remembered when Dorothy realised there was no place like home. He giggled, trying to sound like Dorothy in the old classic film. He tapped his shoes together three times while repeating the sentence.

Jesper Melander loved the innocence of these people inside their new home. He loved their sense of security... the feeling of being home where it is safe, and they feel so untouchable. That was what he dreamt of destroying.

He tilted his head as the lights went out in the bedroom and everything went quiet. Jesper Melander felt the knife in his hand and closed his eyes for just a second, taking in the fresh salty air mixed with the wonderful smells of the anticipation of a kill.

Jesper Melander opened his eyes and looked at the sleeping house. "What a be-ea-u-ti-ful home. I'm never ever leaving again, Auntie Em." Jesper Melander laughed. "Oh, you'll never ever leave this house again."

Jesper Melander walked up to a window in the back leading to the basement. It was slightly ajar. They hadn't been into the basement yet. Of course they hadn't. They had just moved in. They hadn't had time to check all the doors and windows yet. In a new house, people never know where they all are or how many there are, do they? No, they don't.

Jesper Melander slid inside and ended up in an empty room in the basement. Quietly, Jesper Melander found the stairs leading up.

He started chanting about a yellow brick road and lions and tigers, and dancing up the stairs.

Jesper Melander opened the door and walked inside the kitchen. With quick and very determined steps, he walked straight toward the bedroom. The door was open. Jesper Melander stopped by the bed and looked at the happy couple in their sleep. The husband was snoring heavily.

Jesper Melander giggled.

Jesper Melander walked to the husband's side and sat on the edge of the bed. Then, he stroked the man gently on the cheek till he opened his eyes, blinking and trying to see in the darkness.

"W... what?... Maria?"

"No. Not Maria," Jesper Melander whispered. "But I bet you wish I was."

"What the...?"

Jesper Melander lifted the knife into the air and plunged it deep into the husband's chest. Between the ribs. Straight to the heart.

A scream startled him. It came from the wife. She had woken up. Good. Jesper Melander pulled the knife out of the man's chest and blood spurted up from the wound. Jesper Melander then stabbed the husband again, pulled out the knife and stabbed him again, every time pushing the blade in deeper. The body of the husband stiffened in a spasm. Guttural and gurgling sounds escaped his throat, his last effort to try to catch a breath. The woman wouldn't stop screaming in fear. Her eyes were wide with terror. Jesper Melander fed off her anxiety. The woman was screaming her lungs out now. It was like the most beautiful music to Jesper Melander. So soothing. So refreshing to the soul.

"What have you done?!" the woman screamed. "Oh my! Oh my! Jonas! JONAS!"

Jesper Melander took a photographic memory picture of her frozen and wide-eyed state. All the feeling of safety and security she had felt just before going to sleep had been sucked right out of her in a matter of seconds. Her eyes darted back and forth between Jonas and Jesper Melander. Jesper Melander was amused by the display. He tilted his head and giggled. The woman's eyes searched for a way out, and she tried to run for it, but Jesper Melander grabbed her and held her back.

"Please, don't kill me," she whimpered, her lips quivering in despair. "Please, let me go."

Jesper Melander lowered the blade and sliced it into her. The smell of blood was deep in his nostrils. Her begging eyes were pleading to be spared. But it was too late. She fell to the ground in a pool of blood. Jesper Melander giggled again.

"Guess we're not in Kansas anymore. We must be over the rainbow!"

FOUR
JULY 2014

It was one of those rare quiet mornings. The kids were still on their summer break, and Victor had decided to sleep in, for once.

This is a first, I thought as I walked downstairs and he wasn't there.

Usually, he was the first one up, sitting in the kitchen, waiting for his breakfast. I was even late. I had slept till eight-thirty and was certain he would be very anxious... almost on the verge of annoyed that I wasn't there yet.

But, he wasn't. He hadn't even gotten up yet, I realized, when I went back upstairs and checked his room. Victor was still asleep. A very rare and delightful sight.

It had been a tough summer for all of us. Maya had moved back home but was still suffering from amnesia after some lunatic doctor had drugged her as a part of an experiment. I had hoped she would have regained more of her memory by now, but it was still almost the same as when I brought her home before the summer started. Every day, I showed her pictures of her childhood, and every day, she told me she still didn't remember. There were days when I could tell she tried to please me and told me she remembered some of it, but I knew she was lying. It was wearing on all of us, especially Victor, who didn't seem to understand why we were all fussing over Maya now.

"Why does she need to remember all this stuff anyway?" he would say.

He was just upset that I didn't pay as much attention to him as I used to.

There had been some improvement in Maya, though, even if it didn't go as fast as I would have liked it to. She had started to get glimpses of her life in her dreams. If it was just the pictures that caused them to come, I didn't know, but something had happened, and I was so grateful for that, little as it might be.

I had tried to contact every doctor in the country, hoping to get some help, but had received no other advice than what Dr. Faaborg had given me. It was all about giving her rest and time.

I just wanted her to be able to go back to school in August. I wanted her to go back to her old life and to be able to get by like a normal teenager. Heck, I wanted her to yell at me and roll her eyes at me like she used to. It was almost like she had become numb. She was never excited or happy about anything; she wasn't even angry or upset about anything. She was just this ghost-like version of herself.

I had asked the region for help. I tried to get a social worker to provide us with something, anything would do, but the offices were closed for the summer, so they told me to come back in August. Denmark had to be the only country in the world that closed for an entire month because everyone went on holiday. There was nothing that could be done at this time of year. Anything that had to do with the government—which was most things—closed for the summer or was run by only a few people who could make no important decisions. That was just the way it was.

So, here I was on a beautiful Tuesday morning in the

middle of summer, enjoying my coffee, thinking about my life, and worrying about both of my children and how they were going to make it... when someone knocked on the door. I went to open it. Outside, stood a man in a blue uniform that said he was from the Curtain Company. He smiled. Behind him in the street he had parked a red van with the same name on the side of it.

"Mrs. Boegh?"

"No. You have the wrong house. That's next door. They just moved in yesterday," I said, and pointed at my next-door neighbors. Sophia, Jack, and I had walked over there yesterday to bid them welcome. I had even baked my famous buns for them, and Sophia had taken them wine. They seemed like a nice couple but didn't have any children yet. I had hoped for a new friend for Victor.

The man looked at his papers, baffled. "Oh my. You're right. I'm so sorry for disturbing you like this."

"No problem," I said, and closed the door.

When I turned to walk back, Victor was standing right behind me.

He stared at me with upset eyes. "Where is my breakfast?" he asked.

FIVE

APRIL 2009

She had written him a letter. Louise didn't think anything would come of it. *He probably gets tons of mail from women*, she thought on this spring morning a month later, as she ate her toasted bread. Lorianne and Lurifax were sitting on the table, eating out of their bowls, keeping her company. In the background, the TV was on, as usual. Louise had turned the volume down, so she didn't have to hear about all the ugly stuff going on in the world.

"We don't need to hear about war in Afghanistan or starving children in Africa while eating our breakfast, now do we?" she said to her cats and petted Lorianne on the head. The cat spun around while eating her fish.

"No, we don't," Louise answered herself.

She took another bite of her toast and finished her glass of orange juice when she saw him again. She grabbed the remote and turned up the volume. The trial was still on, and Louise had followed it closely.

She watched as Bjarke Lund walked toward the court and the press corps tried with vulturous delight to get a comment from the man they unanimously had declared was a dangerous psychopath.

"Here he comes, kids. You see him? Oh, he's wearing a red shirt today under his leather vest. That's a great color for him, don't you think, kids? Methinks he looks very handsome today, yes, me do. Oh, just look at that piece of man. Look at those hands and arms. Isn't he just adorable? Did he trim his beard a little? Well, I think he did. It looks very good, but I hope he doesn't cut any more off. I like his beard. Makes him look raw and tough. I like him to look tough."

Lorianne answered with a purr, and then placed herself comfortably in Louise's lap. Louise kept petting her, while staring, paralyzed, at the man of her dreams, following his every move until he disappeared inside the courtroom and the doors were closed.

"Ah. It always goes too fast," Louise murmured. "Guess we won't see him until next week then when he has his next court appearance. Good thing Mommy taped all his appearances on TV, isn't it? That way we can watch him over and over again."

Louise got up from her chair and went to get more coffee, when the mail was pushed through her door. She grabbed the letters and went through them.

"Bill... bill... another bill, ah, this is water; better pay that one right away. The others can wait a month or two, I guess. But wait. What is this?"

Louise dropped all the other mail on the floor and studied the white envelope with her name handwritten on the front. Her heart was pounding hard in her chest. On the outside, it had a stamp telling the receiver that its content had been security checked by the police. Louise almost forgot to breathe. She ripped it open and pulled out a handwritten letter. Two pages. Front and back!

Louise couldn't believe her own eyes. She was gasping for air, her hands shaking heavily, as she started to read.

Dear Louise,

Is it okay if I call you Louise? I hope so. After the letter I received from you, I got the feeling it would be all right. Anyway, I am writing to tell you I truly enjoyed your letter and especially the photo of you and your cats. I myself am very much a cat person, and I can tell that Lurifax and Lorianne are two very special cats. They are beautiful. And so are you, Louise. You are a very beautiful woman.

Louise looked up to catch her breath. Her cheeks had gotten warm and red, and she had to sit down to read the rest. She couldn't believe he had actually answered her letter. She couldn't believe he really liked her and thought she was pretty. No one had ever called her pretty before. It was all very exciting.

Louise kept reading the letter and soon realized that she had actually established some sort of connection to the man she hadn't stopped dreaming about since the day she saw him on TV for the first time. In his answer, he wrote that he would very much like to get to know her better, and maybe even get to meet her one day.

I hope to hear from you again soon, Louise. I will be thinking about your kind words to me in your first letter until I do. You seem to be the only one in this world who understands me and believes in my innocence. For that, I am eternally grateful. It makes me believe in humanity again.

Yours truly,

Bjarke Lund

SIX

JULY 2014

Peter Wagn had worked with curtains for twenty-five years. He loved curtains, and he loved being able to help people find the right curtains to fit their needs in their homes. It was a job where he made people happy, and he truly enjoyed that. He got to go to people's houses, and every day was different, every house was different, every person's needs were different.

It was always exciting to meet new customers, and today he was going to do just that. He had the van packed with samples of different kinds of curtains, different colors, different patterns, and different types of fabric. Today, he would sit down, typically with the female in the house, and decide what she wanted for her new home. Then, he would measure the windows, and within a week, he could promise they would have their perfect curtains. That was why the customers came to him. They could easily go buy something and put it up themselves, but people who contacted him wanted something special. They wanted their home to be unique. And that was exactly what he provided... something specially designed and sewn to fit those exact windows. He was a specialist, and his customers got the best treatment.

That's why they came back again and again, and that was why they referred him to their best friends. Peter's wife had thought he was stupid when he decided to start his own company back in the nineties.

"No one uses curtains anymore," she said. "They want blinds. Curtains are outdated."

But he'd proved her wrong, hadn't he? Yes, there were years when business was bad, when he considered expanding to also provide specially designed blinds for his customers, but little by little, people had returned to using curtains, and as it was now considered a luxury to have custom-made curtains made with good quality fabric, Peter's business was blooming like never before. People in Denmark had money, and they wanted luxury. They remodeled their houses, and they didn't compromise on quality anymore.

Peter smiled as he walked toward the front door of his new client. He had very much been looking forward to getting his fingers on this particular house. It was an old brick house, built a century ago. It had huge windows leading to the back garden. He knew it had, because he had often looked at it from the beach side while walking his golden retriever. He had adored those windows for years and dreamt of dressing them in gorgeous silk draperies. He was hoping the new owners would agree.

Peter held his case with the samples and measuring tape in one hand, as he lifted the other to ring the doorbell. He was whistling with joy. He glanced at the old house next door that he had thought was this address. He must have been tired. Plus, in his defense, he had never actually seen the house from this side, only from the beach side.

Peter whistled again and studied the window next to the entrance. It was tall and slim. He knew exactly which curtain would be perfect for it. This was going to be one of the high-lights of his career... and a true moneymaker, if he played his cards right. It was all about buttering up the wife. If he was on good terms with her, the sky was the limit.

Maybe I'll finally be able to afford that trip to Thailand I've always wanted to take.

Yes, that was it. He would take a trip to the land with the best fabrics in the world. But he would go alone. Yes, Annie wouldn't understand; she didn't appreciate the quality of a good fabric like he did. She never had. Peter would find an excuse to go alone.

Why isn't anyone opening the door?

He rang the doorbell again.

Still nothing? Am I too early?

Peter looked at his watch. No, he was right on time as scheduled when Mrs. Boegh called him over the phone. Peter grunted. He realized the front door was slightly ajar. They wouldn't leave it like this if they weren't home. No, not these people. They were good people. Peter had sensed it right away while speaking to Mrs. Boegh on the phone. She sounded like a very intelligent woman.

Maybe Mrs. Boegh was in there somewhere, but simply didn't hear the bell. Maybe the doorbell didn't work. Peter Wagn pushed the door open while knocking on it.

"Hello? Mrs. Boegh?"

Still silence. Peter walked in. He gasped at the sight of the large windows. They were even more spectacular up close. And so tall. And wide. This was going to be very expensive. Maybe he could arrange two trips to Thailand. One this year and one for next year.

"This is Peter Wagn from the Curtain Company. We spoke on the phone. I was supposed to meet you here today. Hello?"

The door to the bedroom was wide open. Peter took a chance and walked inside.

"Mrs. Boegh? Hello?"

That was when he stopped. He had stepped in something.

His shoes made a strange sound. Like they were wet. Peter looked at them. The entire floor was soaked in something. It wasn't water. Peter held his breath. He followed the flood that led inside the bedroom and surrounded the bed. Peter's heart stopped at the sight that met him on top of the bed. He barely had the strength to let out the petrifying scream that was soon heard throughout the entire neighborhood.

SEVEN

JULY 2014

Victor ate his breakfast faster than I had ever seen him. Maya came down and sat at the table.

"Good morning, sweetheart. Did you sleep well?" I said in a much higher-pitched tone than expected. It was strange how hard it had become for me to act like myself around her. Why couldn't I just relax? Why did I feel like I had to be so extra attentive, extra protective, extra... well, everything around her?

"She's not going to break," my mom had said to me the other day. "She's not an expensive porcelain statue."

It was spot-on, but I didn't tell her. It was exactly how I felt. Like Maya was so fragile she could break if I said something wrong. The truth was, I simply had no idea how to act around her.

"Fine," Maya replied, emotionless.

I forced a smile. "Good. I'm glad to hear it. What would you like for breakfast? Cereal or buttered toast? I have buns from yesterday, if you'd like."

Maya shrugged. "I don't know."

You don't know? You always know exactly what you want, Maya. You don't like my cooking, remember? It's too unhealthy.

Don't you remember? Where are you? Who are you, and what have you done with my daughter?

"I'll toast some bread for you then."

"Okay."

Okay? Oh my. You used to fight me on this constantly. The first three things I would suggest, you'd wrinkle your little freckled nose and tell me no. Now, all you say is okay and I don't know. Please, just fight me on this.

I bit my lip and looked at her. Her eyes were so empty, so emotionless. She tried to smile, but it came off awkward.

Give it time, Emma. Give her time. It'll come back. She'll come back eventually.

I put the bread in the toaster and found some cheese in the fridge. I poured her a glass of juice and put it in front of her.

"Thanks," she said, and drank.

I grabbed the photo album and sat next to her. She looked at it, and I could tell it scared her to have to go through it again.

"Just a few pictures," I said. "We need to do a little every day. School is starting soon, and... well, I don't know what's going to happen, to be honest, but you need to at least know your family."

"I think I know them by now," she said.

"Their names. Yes. You know all their names, but you don't really know them, do you?"

You have no idea how much they love you, do you? Don't you even remember their love for you? Don't you remember how much you love us?

I grabbed her hand in mine. I could tell she was a little anxious. It was hard on her every time. But it had to be done. I opened the book and let her look at pictures of herself, then with me, then with her father and Victor. She forced a smile and went through them, nodding.

"I know these people. Dad has even been here to visit me, remember? I know all I need to know about them."

The bread popped up in the toaster and I went to get it. I put a piece of cheese on top of it and put it on the table in front of Maya. She grabbed it and ate.

Without even a wrinkle of the nose. You hate that kind of cheese, Maya. You don't like it, and now you're eating it like you've been eating it all your life. How, Maya? How am I going to make you remember who you are?

I stood by the sink and looked out the window while Maya ate and drank. I pressed back my tears, as I had done so many mornings before this. I wanted to cry, I wanted to yell. Hell, I wanted to scream at my daughter to make her remember. All the other mornings, I had done the dishes in silence, praying quietly that this would be the day when Maya came back to me. But, this day, I was done being quiet. I felt the frustration plant itself throughout my body, and I opened my mouth to just let it out.

But someone beat me to it.

EIGHT

JULY 2014

"What was that?" Maya asked, for the first time showing some sort of emotion: fear.

Victor didn't even look up from his cereal.

"I don't know," I said, startled. "It sounded like it came from next door." I looked out the window and saw the Curtain Company's red van parked outside in the driveway. The street was empty. Everything seemed quiet.

"I don't know," I repeated. "Maybe someone was hurt in there. Maybe the curtain guy fell off his ladder or something."

I bit my lip, wondering if I should go over there and check to see if they were all right. But, then again, he probably wasn't alone in there. The nice couple had to be there.

I returned to my dishes with a strange, unsettled feeling. The scream didn't sound like someone getting hurt. It sounded like someone was afraid. Not just afraid. More like terrified. I turned on the tap and started washing the pan from last night's dinner. I couldn't escape this strange feeling that something was terribly wrong. I looked out the window again, but the street remained calm.

I turned my head to look at my kids. Should I just go and

check on the neighbors? I would want to know that my neighbors were looking out for me, wouldn't I?

But, I didn't want to come off like a nosy neighbor either.

"Only bad witches are ugly."

"What was that, Victor?" I asked. I looked at my son. He had stopped eating, but still wasn't looking at me.

"It's from *The Wizard of Oz*," Maya suddenly exclaimed. She clapped her hand over her mouth. "Oh my. I remember something. Mom, I remember the film. I remember watching it with Grandpa when I was six. You and Dad were away for the weekend, remember? Now, where did you go?"

I stared, baffled, at my daughter. I was about to break down and cry. I forgot everything else.

Her eyes met mine. "Berlin, right? You brought us back that hideous porcelain sculpture that's still in my room."

"The one that was supposed to be Winnie-the-Pooh, but you thought he looked scary."

"You had to hide it at night because it gave me nightmares. Mom, I remember. I remembered something!"

Maya had tears in her eyes, and so did I. Victor was still staring at the table. I sat in a chair next to my daughter and grabbed her hand. I felt so overwhelmed with emotions, I was about to explode.

"*The Wizard of Oz*, huh?" I said. "Maybe we should watch it later today. Would that be good?"

"Yes, Mom," Maya said. "I would very much like that."

"MOM!" It was Victor who was now yelling. He rose to his feet and held his hands to both his ears.

"What is it, honey?" His body was shaking. This was serious. "What's wrong, baby?"

"She's wearing the shoes. She's wearing the ruby red slippers!"

I looked at Maya. "More *Wizard of Oz* stuff?" I asked. I

hadn't seen the film since I was a child, but I did remember the shoes.

She nodded. I looked at Victor again. It seemed very urgent, and I got to thinking about the scream coming from next door. Victor had this special gift of sensing things that no one else did. Maybe that was what this was. Maybe he was telling me something.

"She's wearing the shoes, Mommy. She's wearing the shoes!"

I got up from my chair and threw my apron on the table. "Stay here. Maya, you're in charge while I'm gone."

NINE

JULY 2014

I ran into the street and toward my new neighbor's house with my heart pounding hard in my chest. Victor was never wrong about these things. He knew before the rest of us, and I had to take him seriously. Even if I felt a little stupid and risked being the most annoying neighbor from now on.

I stormed to the front door and saw that it was open. I knocked on it, as I walked inside. "Hello?"

No answer.

"Hello? This is Emma Frost. Your next-door neighbor. I thought I heard something, and thought I'd stop by to..."

The house was so quiet, I doubted anyone was even in here. But I had seen the curtain van outside the house and the couple's car was in the driveway. There had to be someone in here, right?

I had a bad feeling as I walked into the living room, only to find it empty. I continued into the kitchen, then the bedroom.

Then I stopped.

The sight was too gruesome to bear. I felt like the walls of the room were closing in on me and I was suffocating. What the hell was this? Blood was everywhere. The floor was soaked in it, the white bed sheets were soaked in it, and it was dripping from the bed onto the floor. The walls were sprayed with blood. On top of the bed lay two mutilated bodies, which I recognized as the couple from yesterday. They were both naked, and the woman was wearing a pair of glittering ruby red slippers.

She's wearing the shoes. She's wearing the ruby red slippers!

On the floor next to the bed, a pair of legs stuck out. They were dressed in a dark blue pair of trousers.

The curtain guy! He's moving. He's alive!

I rushed toward him. He was still fully dressed but lying with his face in the blood.

"Sir? Are you all right?" I asked and turned him around. He groaned. I kneeled next to him. "Are you okay?"

"What... what happened?"

"I think you fainted."

He opened his eyes wide. "Oh my God! The bodies!"

He tried to get up but became dizzy and fell back into my lap. His hair was smeared with the blood from the floor. Now, it was all over my trousers and my hands.

"They're still there," I said, trying hard to calm myself down.

Don't panic. The worst thing you can do now is panic. Stay calm. You have to stay calm and focused.

"Stay down," I said, feeling slightly lightheaded myself.

Remember to breathe. If you stop breathing, if you hyperventilate, you'll faint too. Keep breathing.

I found my phone in my pocket and called Morten, my boyfriend and a police officer on the island. My voice was shaking heavily as we spoke.

"You need to come. Something terrible has happened."

I fought to keep the tears back. I took a deep breath to calm myself.

"Where are you?"

"They just moved in, Morten. They just bought the house

and now... now they're gone. It's my neighbors, Morten. It happened right next to us. While we were in our house. It could have been us. Why did this happen to them, Morten? They were nice people. They seemed so nice."

"Emma, you're rambling. I'm in my car now. Tell me. Are you in your neighbor's house? Is that it? Is that where I need to go? Talk to me."

I was breathing heavily now. I found it hard to focus. The room was spinning. The curtain guy was groaning.

"We need the doctor too. There's a guy who fainted."

"Okay, I'll make the call. What else, Emma? What happened to your neighbors? Where are they?"

"They're... they're... they're on the bed. There's a lot of blood, Morten. A lot."

Morten went quiet. I heard him take a deep breath as well. "Okay. So... so you believe they're dead? Emma?"

"I'm nodding," I said, sobbing. "They were so young, Morten. They'd just gotten married. Just bought their first house. Who would do such a thing? They had their whole lives ahead of them. They were supposed to have children soon. They were considering it, they told me when I asked. Who...? Why?"

"We can't answer that now, Emma. They were new to the island. We don't know anything about these people. I'm parking outside the house now. I'll keep you on the phone till I see you. Now, where in the house are you?"

"The bedroom."

TEN

JULY 2014

The numerologist sat behind the wheel of her old Toyota, keeping an eye on the house across the street. She had been sitting there every day for nearly a week now, keeping up with Emma Frost's daily routines and writing everything she did in her little notebook.

This morning was particularly active for the dear author in the big house. Usually, it was her children who kept her busy, that and the few hours of writing she managed to squeeze in between chores. But today was different. Today, the numerologist had seen Emma storm into the neighbor's house. She had a feeling she knew what Emma was going to find in there, because the numerologist had been sleeping in her car ever since she started the stakeout, and she had seen someone leave the house next door very late last night. A man with a ponytail and a leather vest. The numerologist had detected a bad aura surrounding the man and knew something was off. He had hurried away, walking with his head bowed, like he didn't want to be seen, and with a smirk on his face that the numerologist had recognized. Whatever he had done in there, he had enjoyed it immensely. No doubt about it.

Not that she cared. Not even when she heard the scream. She wasn't there to keep an eye on those neighbors. No, she was there to spy on Emma Frost, the woman who had ruined everything for her.

There were a couple of people on the numerologist's list. But Emma was the one who the numerologist really wanted to kill.

Now, Emma Frost's annoying boyfriend, who, by the way, had also made the numerologist's list, drove into the driveway in the island's only police car, and hurried inside. The numerologist followed him with her binoculars and noted in her book once he was inside. A few minutes later, the island's only doctor arrived with messy hair and his bag in hand.

"The house number is thirty-eight... ouch," she mumbled. "Well, bad things were bound to happen in this place, I guess. They had it coming. Too bad people are so ignorant when it comes to the power of numbers. When will they ever learn?"

The numerologist grabbed a cracker from her bag and ate it while waiting for Emma Frost to come back out of the neighbor's house. She took out another cracker and took a bite. Misty was fussing in the passenger seat.

"What's up with you?" the numerologist asked.

The rat looked at her. Its long whiskers were vibrating.

"Oh, you're hungry too. Of course," the numerologist said, and handed the cracker to the rat. "It's been a long night for the both of us."

The rat nibbled the cracker. It made the numerologist chuckle. Misty was so cute, so adorable with her brown eyes and pointy nose.

Once the rat was done taking its bite, the numerologist finished the rest of the cracker. She washed it down with some orange juice and threw the empty bottle on the floor. The car was filled with rubbish, and she knew she would need to clean it up soon.

She watched as Misty plunged into the sea of rubbish on the floor. Then, she smiled. Misty was having such fun with it. Maybe later, she thought. She was, after all, almost done with her intensive surveillance. She had taken so many notes on Emma Frost's whereabouts during the last week that she was now ready for the next move. It was all about getting to know Emma's weak spots, finding out where she was vulnerable, and the numerologist had found just that. She and Misty would soon go back to the small room they had rented at an old nasty lady's house and prepare for round two.

ELEVEN
APRIL 2009

They put him away. Louise could hardly believe what she had heard on TV. The judge had found Bjarke guilty of killing his girlfriend and her two children, who were seven and nine years old.

It's just not right, Louise thought. *He told me himself that he didn't do it. I believe him. Why didn't they?*

She had written him back, and he had asked her to call him on the phone. He was allowed to make and receive calls. They had talked for an hour. That was as long as he was allowed to. He had explained to her that he was devastated. That he was innocent and had no idea what happened to his ex-girlfriend Rikke and her sons.

"They haven't even found their bodies," he said. "I don't know why they think I killed them."

"Why, this is outrageous," Louise had said. "You can't go to prison for something you didn't do. It's not fair."

"Well, the world isn't always fair, now is it?" Bjarke replied.

He was right, she thought. He was so smart, it startled her. "But they don't even know if they're dead or not," she argued.

"Maybe they just left the country, or maybe they're hiding somewhere."

"I don't know where they are," he answered. "And, to be honest, I don't know what to do. They said they found blood in the house, but that could have been from one of the boys hurting himself. That happened all the time. I loved them, Louise. You must know that. I really loved them."

"I believe you. I believe you loved them."

"I feel so alone. No one wants to hear my side of the story. It's like they don't even care."

"I care. I want to hear it," Louise said.

Bjarke took a deep breath. Louise felt like he was so close at that moment and held the phone tighter.

"I know you do. I'm so grateful for that. I can't tell you how much it helps to know that I have you. Please, don't leave me. Everybody leaves me. My mom, my girlfriend, my friends, everyone."

"I won't," Louise said. She could feel his loneliness and it almost made her cry. How could they ever think that sweet man would kill anyone? Just from talking to him, she knew he could never have done any of all those horrible things they accused him of.

"You know they think I killed my mother as well, right? They just didn't have enough evidence to convict me. That's what they say... that they now, finally, have me."

Louise bit her lip. She believed him. But the thing about the mother bothered her. "What... what happened to her, anyway?"

A deep sigh followed. Louise was afraid she had gone too far. "You don't... you don't have to answer that," she continued.

"No, no. It's okay," he said.

Louise felt relieved. She didn't want to lose him.

"To be perfectly honest with you, and I have a feeling that I can be perfectly honest, am I right?"

"Yes. Yes, you can. Of course. I'm here to listen," Louise said, fearing slightly what would come next. She wanted him to be innocent. She believed he was. Of everything.

"I think she killed herself," Bjarke said. "I mean, they never found her, but I think she might have walked down to the lake and drowned herself. She threatened to do so on several occasions when I was growing up. One day, she was simply gone. I came home from work... I was working at an auto shop at the time, learning to fix cars and thought that was what I was supposed to do with my life, you know? Then, bam, my life changed forever. My mom wasn't at the house and her sister accused me of having killed her. She never liked me much. She thought I was dangerous. I have no idea why she felt that way. I had never harmed a fly up until that point. But my aunt always thought I had ruined my mother's life... that I was to blame for the way her life turned out or something. I don't know. But she blamed it all on me and told the police I had threatened to kill my mom several times. Then they found the axe in the garage that had my fingerprints on it. But, of course, it did; I mean, I used it to chop wood for our fireplace. I helped my mom in every way I could, you know? There was some blood on the axe too they claimed, but it was mine. They said I lucked out. They never believed for one second that I could be innocent. Can you imagine that? Can you imagine having to fight for people to believe you like that?"

Louise thought long and hard but had to realize she had no idea how that felt. She had never been in a position like that. To her, Bjarke was so experienced in life; he was so smart... and so misunderstood. It was all just a series of very unfortunate events.

Now, she looked at the TV screen while the reporter told the viewers that Bjarke Lund had been sentenced to spend sixteen years behind bars.

The reporter also said that Bjarke Lund immediately

appealed the judgment to a higher court, but there wasn't much chance that it would accept the appeal.

"In my opinion, there's no doubt about it," the reporter finished the piece. "Bjarke Lund is going away for a very long time."

TWELVE
JULY 2014

I was devastated, to put it mildly. Morten arrived at the house, and soon after, Dr. Williamsen stormed into the bedroom, looking perplexed and confused.

Morten was still looking at the victims as the doctor entered.

"Oh my," the doctor exclaimed when he saw the bodies. He held his chest with his left hand and dropped the brown bag that had been in his right.

"You can say that again," Morten said. I could tell he was holding back his desire to cry. He had seen several murder victims in his life, but I knew it hurt every time.

"This man is alive," I said, and pointed at the curtain guy, who still had his head in my lap.

The doctor looked at me. He was sweating heavily. The curtain guy moaned.

"He fainted when he saw the bodies. I think he might have bumped his head on the bed or something when he fell," I said. "There seems to be a bruise over here, but it's hard to tell how bad it is with all the blood he has smeared on his face and in his hair. Most of it doesn't belong to him."

"I see," Dr. Williamsen said. "Let me take a look."

"I think I can sit up now," the curtain guy, who had told me his name was Peter Wagn, said.

"It's okay," the doctor said.

Peter Wagn sat up. I got up on my feet and looked at Morten, while Dr. Williamsen took a look at Peter Wagn's bruise.

"This isn't too bad," I heard the doctor say, then I walked closer to Morten. I wanted him to hold me, but I didn't want to get too close to the bloody scene. All I really wanted was to get the heck out of there.

"What's with the shoes?" I asked. "What do you make of that?"

Morten shrugged. "I have no idea. But be careful not to touch anything. I've called the coroners. They'll be here in a couple of hours, hopefully. They'll tell us what we need to know."

There was silence. The doctor told Peter Wagn to stand up and showed him three fingers and asked him how many he saw. Peter Wagn seemed to be better already, I thought. I couldn't believe I had almost ignored the scream.

I looked at the woman on the bed. She was gorgeous. So young. Maybe in her twenties, I thought. She'd never experienced the joy of having children. I couldn't imagine a worse fate. It took all I had to not cry... to not lose my grip. I threw a glance around the room and spotted a pair of gold earrings on the dresser, an iPad on a small end table, and the guy's wallet next to it. It wasn't a robbery gone wrong. This was a kill, a brutal and bloody kill, and my experience with killers told me that whoever had done it seemed to have enjoyed it.

The sparkling shoes gave me the chills. It told me it was planned. It was sick. These young innocent people had been in the prime of their lives.

"Let me take you home," Morten said. "You need to get some rest."

I nodded. He put his arm around me as we walked out. The smell of blood was still in my nostrils as we went outside. I took a deep breath to try to remove it. Morten walked me back to the house and helped me inside. Victor and Maya were still in the kitchen.

"What was it, Mom?" Maya asked. Her eyes were wide and fearful. "What was the screaming?"

I looked at Victor, who was still staring at the table. I had no idea what to tell them. I didn't want them to worry. They both had enough on their minds. Especially Victor, whose mind never seemed to take a break. "The police are taking care of everything, kids," Morten said. "No need to worry. We've got it under control. There's nothing to be afraid of. The neighbors had a little accident, but it's all taken care of."

I stared at Morten and was surprised at his ability to lie like that. At first, I didn't think they would buy it, but they did. Maya relaxed, and Victor got up and ran into the garden to play with his trees.

Morten kissed my forehead. "I better get back. Probably going to work on this all day. I'll see if I can be here for dinner, all right?"

"Sounds good to me," I said. "Maybe cooking will help take my mind off of this."

Morten looked into my eyes. "Are you sure you're all right? Do you want me to call for your parents?"

"They're in Copenhagen for the week. A little romantic getaway, they called it."

"Still madly in love, I take it?" Morten asked.

"You wouldn't believe it."

"Good for them."

"Yeah. Guess so." I looked into his eyes. I really loved him, but it had been awhile since I had felt madly in love with him.

Right at this moment, I was too shocked to feel any other emotion than terror.

He kissed my forehead again. It made me feel like a child. "I better get back. Take care of yourself," he said.

"You too. See you later."

THIRTEEN
JULY 2014

I tried hard not to but couldn't help crying. I sat in the kitchen with my coffee most of the morning, wondering about the nice couple I had met so briefly the day before. Victor was playing in the garden, while Maya had gone to her room to be on the computer. I told her to go through all her old pictures in the computer and on her phone and iPad. It was the first time in my life I had actually asked my child to go on Facebook and Twitter. She hadn't wanted to go out since we got back, nor had she texted any of her friends yet. But now that she suddenly remembered something from her childhood, she had gained new hope, and so had I.

Plus, it kept her busy, so she didn't ask more questions about what was going on next door. The driveway and area in front of the neighbor's house had turned into quite the scene.

The coroners had arrived from Copenhagen and parked their blue vans outside, and it had, little by little, gathered a crowd outside the police blockage. People were talking loudly, asking questions, and spreading rumors about what might be going on.

I heard someone walk past my window telling someone else

that she had heard that there had been a fire in the house; the other replied that she heard it was a suicide. The island's TV station was present as well, the reporter and the photographer trying frantically to get a comment from one of the officers working the scene. I even saw a journalist and a photographer from the mainland, from one of the national newspapers. They knew it was something big. I had no idea how people like that always managed to know, but they did. Soon, it would make the headlines all over the country.

It didn't take long before it did. Early in the afternoon, I grabbed my laptop and scrolled through some of the tabloid papers, and it was already plastered all over their front pages.

COUPLE SLAUGHTERED IN THEIR NEW HOME
A NIGHT OF JOY TURNED TO NIGHT OF TERROR

I sighed and scrolled through the articles. I hated this. Somewhere out there, the killer was probably doing the exact same thing... going through the articles about what he'd done, about his accomplishments, enjoying every word of it.

I had known my share of killers, and this one didn't seem to be any different. The brutality was remarkable though.

I poured myself another cup of coffee and was staring out the window at the scene, when I spotted Sophia. She was walking toward my house. A second later, she walked inside my front door.

"Have you heard about it?"

She took one glance at me, and then smiled compassionately.

"Of course you have. Geez. What a show out there, huh? I can't believe they're dead. I mean they just moved in yesterday. It's crazy."

"I know. Coffee?"

"Definitely," Sophia said and sat down. "Make it Irish. I need it. This affair creeps me out."

I chuckled and found a bottle of whiskey. I poured some in both of our cups. I served it to her and sat down as well.

"Can you believe it?" Sophia said again, after sipping her coffee. "Right in there. Right next to your house, someone was brutally murdered. Probably while we were all asleep. What do you make of it, Emma?"

I shrugged and drank. "I have no idea. But, then again, we didn't know these people. They might have owed money to someone, or maybe they were freaking drug dealers."

"So, you think it was, like, a job? Like a hit man or something?" Sophia asked.

"I'm just saying we don't know," I said.

"Why didn't he just shoot them, then? Don't hit men have big guns that they run around scaring people with?"

"I don't know, Sophia," I said, smiling at her wonderful childish approach to things. Sophia did watch a lot of films and TV shows. "Maybe someone was setting an example. Sending out a message of some sort. We don't know. But, they did buy one of the most expensive houses on the island, and that's a lot for such a young couple, don't you think?"

"Yeah. You're probably right. They have to have been drug dealers or something. Maybe the mob?" Sophia looked almost excited.

"Let's not get carried away here. Maybe they just borrowed money from the wrong people."

Sophia scoffed. "That would have had to have been some really wrong people if they ended up like this. I mean, a little punching them around might have done the trick."

"Mmm..." I said pensively.

"I think I know what you're thinking." Sophia said. "You're thinking, let's find out, aren't you?"

I shrugged again and sipped my coffee. "Maybe. But then

again, maybe we should just leave it alone. It's really none of our business."

"The hell it isn't," Sophia said. "It's all our business. This is our street. This is our island. This is where our children are going to grow up—and, hopefully, they will soon, 'cause they're driving me crazy these days. But anyway, I know for myself that I won't be able to close an eye tonight. If I knew that this was just because these people messed with the wrong crowd, then I could sleep tight at night again, 'cause then they had it coming, but, if not... then..."

"Then what? You'll never sleep again?" I asked.

Sophia pushed the computer toward me. "Let's just say we have a new situation then. But you have the skills. You can hack or crack or hike your way into these people's lives and give me my sleep back. So, get to it, sister. I'm counting on you."

"First of all, it's not at all as easy as you make it sound. I mean, I guess I could check their bank account, and maybe even get access to their network and computer, if they had the time to set it up, before they..."

I paused and felt awful again. This was terrible, and what Sophia was asking me to do was bad. It really wasn't any of our business.

"So, you could know all about them in just a few hours, couldn't you?" Sophia asked. She looked excited. It made me feel even worse. Like a vulture.

"Look, it's not like we're going to rob them or anything," Sophia said. "I just want certainty. I want to know. And I sure can't wait for that useless police force of ours to find out. I need to know as soon as possible. Aren't you the least bit curious?"

I was. I was very curious about who these people were, but to go through their personal stuff only hours after they had been killed, just seemed a little... well a little... no, a lot... it was just so wrong.

Sophia gave me her puppy-dog eyes, and I laughed. Mostly

because she was anything but an innocent puppy. I loved her dearly, but that she was not. It felt good to laugh though. Made me feel better.

Sophia pushed the computer closer to me. "Come on. I know you want to. It's calling to you. Can you hear it?" Sophia moved the lid of my laptop to make it look like it was a giant mouth speaking. "Use me, Emma. Use me to find ease. You know you want to. Use the gift. You have the gift. Use it."

I chuckled. "Okay, then. Just don't tell any of our neighbors. I don't want them thinking I might snoop in their affairs as well."

FOURTEEN

MAY 2009

Louise was nervous. She had this tickling sensation in her stomach while sitting on the train from Esbjerg to Copenhagen. Herstedvester Prison was located in Albertslund, just outside of the capital. This was the place where they put all the most dangerous prisoners in Denmark.

Louise had never visited a prison before. It was all very exciting and a little scary. But he would be there. And she was looking so much forward to finally seeing him in real life. Up until now, they had been writing letters to each other every week, and she already felt like she knew him better than she had known any man in her life. And he had gotten to know her as well. He really wanted to. He really liked her, he wrote in almost every letter. And he wanted to get to know her better. He wanted to know everything about her. No one had ever wanted to know about Louise before. No boys in school or men later in her life had ever wanted to date her or anything. Not even back when she worked cleaning the kitchen at the senior center, a job the city had found for her.

To many people, Louise came off as a little odd. She knew that, and always kept her distance from them. She was different.

She even had the doctor's word for it. She had a condition that she couldn't remember the name of, but they told her it meant she would never be mentally older than a fifteen-year-old. It was okay for her. She didn't mind, and as long as she took her medicine, she was fine. The city had given her rehabilitation when she was just twenty-three, and after that, she never had to work again, they told her. She didn't completely understand why she didn't have to work at the kitchen anymore, but she enjoyed staying home with her cats, so she didn't complain.

The train rushed across the countryside, and after two hours, she was in Copenhagen, where she found a bus to Albertslund. She had planned the route from home, as it had been many years since she was last in the capital, and it was so easy to get lost.

Her mom and dad didn't know she was going to visit Bjarke. She had told them over the phone that she was corresponding with him, and it had made them so angry with her. But she didn't care. What did they know about being young and being in love?

"For the first time, someone actually likes me," she told them. She was disappointed to learn that they weren't as happy about this as she was.

"But he's a very dangerous man," her mother pleaded. "Please stay away from him."

"He's not dangerous, Mother. I know him. He is nice. He is innocent. He never killed anyone."

"Don't be naïve," her mother snorted.

"I'm not," she had said, and hung up the phone. Her parents were so annoying. They always thought they got to decide everything. For once in her life, Louise wanted to be in charge. She loved this man, and she was so thrilled to go and see him. No one should get in the way of her happiness. So, she decided to simply not tell them. They would just try to stop her.

On the bus, Louise felt the tickling sensation in her stomach again. At the age of thirty-eight, this wasn't a sensation she felt often. It was her last chance if she was ever going to meet someone. And now she had. Maybe he wasn't going to be able to be there for her and live with her like other men, but it didn't matter. He was nice and he liked her. What more did she need?

The bus stopped in front of a huge building and the driver told Louise this was her stop. She got out and stared at the enormous brick wall surrounding the buildings. Again, she felt the butterflies, and she couldn't help but chuckle. She found her ID and walked toward the entrance.

This is it. The moment has finally arrived. In there, somewhere on the other side of these thick walls is the man of my dreams waiting for me. Just for me.

Louise could hardly contain her excitement.

FIFTEEN

JULY 2014

"These kids had no money!"

I looked at Sophia who had probably hoped for more exciting news. It turned out to be easier than I thought to get access to the couple's lives. People really weren't being very careful about protecting their private information. I'd gained access to the Boegh's online bank within an hour.

"Really?" Sophia asked. "How did they afford this house, then?"

"Big loan. They were in over their heads, the way I see it. It's not hard to see that buying this house was going to eventually give them trouble. They both had good incomes, but this house was expensive, and they even took another loan to cover the moving costs. They were really going to be living tight. They also have another loan to cover the costs of their wedding. These people weren't being very smart about their money. That's for sure."

"Looks like they were a little unrealistic. So, they might have taken other loans outside of the bank, then?" Sophia asked. "Maybe they owed money all over the place?"

"Hmm, they might," I said, and looked at the screen. "He

was a lawyer, though. Doesn't sound like something a lawyer would do, does it?"

"Anyone can be an idiot with money. Believe me," Sophia said with a loud laugh. "I've met many men who seemed to have it all together on the outside but were fools when it came to money. It doesn't matter what your title is. Anyone can get a gambling debt."

"Definitely. But that's not something I can see here. There are no big transactions of money within the last five years, or anything else suspicious, as far as I can see. But that doesn't tell us anything."

"What else?" Sophia asked.

I tapped on the keyboard. "Well, I did some background on both of them. The woman, Maria Boegh, grew up with her mother, who was on social welfare. They used to live in Vejle on the mainland. I found her files, and she was diagnosed with a lot of stuff—paranoia, social anxiety, and so on—nothing much to note there. The father left when she was just a young child. I found him in Esbjerg, where he is a real estate agent."

"What about the guy?" Sophia asked.

"He came from a more solid background. His father was a farmer. Jonas Boegh grew up on a farm outside of Herning on the mainland as well."

"Farmer? That's some jump from farmer boy to lawyer boy," Sophia exclaimed.

"I guess. Probably just didn't want to end up like his parents, constantly doing hard manual labor. Who knows? Anyway, this doesn't tell us much. It's all pretty ordinary."

Sophia leaned back in her chair and put her arms behind her head. My stomach was hurting from too much coffee, and the empty pot on the counter was a sign that we had been at this all day. I looked at the clock and realized it was time for me to start cooking dinner.

I opened the fridge and took out the roast rump I was going

to make. I found garlic and smeared it all over it. Sophia looked at the computer screen with a disappointed look.

"I told you it wasn't as simple as you thought it would be," I said.

"I know. I just really wanted there to be something. Something that told me why these people had to be brutally massacred in their new home. Something that told me they weren't going to come after my kids or me next. You know what I mean? I don't like this unease I'm feeling."

"Me either," I said with a sigh. "Well, maybe Morten can tell us more once he gets here. If he ever gets here."

"Oh, he will," Sophia said. "For your roast rump, he'd walk to the end of the earth."

I chuckled. "I sure hope you're right."

I found a bag of potatoes and poured them into the sink. I started peeling them, but my thoughts wouldn't leave me alone.

"Did you check this guy's emails?" Sophia asked.

"Yeah, I skimmed through them, why?"

"'Cause he received a threatening letter just two weeks ago."

I stopped peeling, wiped my hands on a tea towel, and approached the computer. Sophia pointed at the screen. "See here. This guy is really mad at him. Calls him all kinds of bad things."

"You're right," I said, and read the message. The email address it was sent from was a Hotmail, and it was simply signed by Furious.

SIXTEEN

JULY 2014

"He was a lawyer, Emma. They get all kinds of threatening mail. Especially when they win a big case like he had just done."

Morten looked at me over the steam from the potatoes. Sophia had left to be with her own family, so now it was just the four of us. Once Maya and Victor were done eating, I pulled out the email that I had printed out.

"You said he had won a case?" I asked and took another piece of the roast. It was so good, I had to have seconds... and probably thirds as well. "What kind of a case was that?"

"I spoke to his firm today, and they said he won a case for this young rich guy whose Dad hired them to get the son free of charges against him. Allegedly, he had raped a girl at his boarding school. The girl had three witnesses who saw what happened, but still, Jonas Boegh got the boy off. He tore their evidence apart, one by one, his boss told me. A work of art, he called it. Probably made some enemies in doing so though."

"So, you don't think it's worth investigating?" I asked, with my mouth full of hot potatoes. How come they always managed to stay this hot, even long after I cooked them? I drank some water to cool my mouth down.

"Of course it is," Morten said. "But right now, there are a lot of things to consider." Morten looked tired. "I'm afraid I'm in a little over my head here. We've only four officers at our station, and they're actually talking about making cutbacks. I have no idea how to deal with this case."

"Aren't you getting help from the mainland?" I asked. I couldn't believe they were actually considering cutting back on the island's already small police department. There had been talk before of cutting it down to just one officer, but that was outrageous to me. It didn't feel very safe to be out here on this small island if something really bad happened.

"They don't have any teams to help us. They're tied up on other cases or taking compensatory time off because of too much overtime. The entire Danish police force is bleeding. There's not enough money. It's as simple as that."

"So, they're expecting you to investigate the case or what?"

"I'll know more tomorrow, when I go to the mainland to our district chief," he said.

"I can't believe they would do that to you."

"It's not something they do to me. They just haven't any other options right now. Like I said, I'm having a meeting with the chief tomorrow, and then we'll see."

I felt frustrated. Knowing Morten, I knew he would be too nice to say what was really on his heart. He would never stand up to them... or ask for help. He was much too proud.

"Well, maybe I'll come with you," I said.

Morten looked up from his plate. "You? Why?"

"Moral support. We can call it a romantic getaway, if you like. Besides, I think we should pay that guy a visit," I said, and tapped on the letter. "He sounds like he really hated Jonas Boegh."

"Calling someone bad words isn't exactly the same as wanting to kill them," Morten said.

"It's a little more than just a few bad words," I said. "He tells him that he better sleep with one eye open from now on. I would call that a threat. Wouldn't you?"

Morten looked pensive. "They were killed at night while in bed." He nodded. "It's worth taking a look at."

I rubbed my leg against his under the table. "Maya is old enough to take care of Victor for a few hours while we're gone. I could be your sexy assistant, your sexy sidekick."

I really liked the idea of spending some time with Morten like this. We hadn't had any time alone together for a really long time. Something was always in the way. Mostly, it was our kids. Morten's daughter Jytte had started wanting to have her dad around more. He had given up on finding the strange doctor who had held Maya captive and come back to the island, so she had asked him to stay home more and more often. She wanted him to take her to films and to watch TV with her at night, and Morten seemed to enjoy her sudden urge to be with her father. In the beginning, I thought it was great, but little by little, I realized that it meant I didn't get to see him as much anymore. I was starting to suspect that she was doing this in order to keep him away from me. I had met her a few times and got the feeling she really didn't like me. I had suggested, several times, that we do something together, all three of us, or all five of us, bringing my kids in as well, but every time, Morten told me, "Not this time, babe. Jytte wants to be alone with her dad. She's not ready yet." It was beginning to irritate me how much of our life she controlled by acting like this. It was like a tap. She could turn it on and off as she pleased, while I had no say in it at all. If she called him, he would go running right away. He never said no to her, and always chose her over me. I was afraid that we were drifting apart, so I wanted to take this opportunity and spend the day with my boyfriend. Plus, I was getting more and more curious about this case, and I wanted to help Morten with the investigation. Maybe even get material for a new book? I was almost done with the one I was writing now. *Easy as One, Two, Three* was going to hit the shops in a few months. I only had to revise it. I needed some new material.

Once we were done eating, Morten grabbed his coat and put it on.

"You're not spending the night?"

"Sorry. Have to get home to the little one."

The little one? She's seventeen!

I stood on my tiptoes and kissed him as he was about to leave. He put his arms around me.

"So, may I come tomorrow?"

Morten smiled. He brushed a lock of hair away from my face. "You can come, but you can't play police officer. You'll have to stay in the car while I talk to this guy."

I kissed him again and whispered, "Deal."

SEVENTEEN

JULY 2014

They had no doubt in their minds. Jacob and Christine walked through the living room, the sound of their shoes echoing off the bare walls. They didn't have to say anything. They knew each other well enough to be able to just share a glance, and then know that they both agreed.

This was it. This was the house they wanted.

Nobody spoke while walking through the three bedrooms of the house. Jacob had taken the morning off to be able to see the house with his wife. He missed an important meeting, but no longer regretted his decision. The real estate agent spoke eagerly and still hadn't seen by the look in their eyes that meant she didn't have to try so hard anymore. The decision had been made. It had been from the moment they entered the house on Niels Sørensens Vej next to Nordby Church.

This was, by far, the most adorable house Christine had ever been in. The ceilings were low, and the roof thatched. The house was built in 1808. It was red, and everything about it was just so endearing. Even the street outside was lovely. It was so narrow that only one car at a time could pass. People were biking, and most were walking. Christine had even seen a horse cart while driving there.

It was more idyllic than she had dared to hope for.

"So, this is basically it," the real estate agent said, smiling, as she finished the tour of the house. "Everything is newly renovated, but, of course, you must keep in mind that a house of this age demands a lot of love and care every year."

"Naturally," Jacob said.

Christina grabbed his hand and dragged him to the window. "We could fit a small swing set over there in the corner for Emilie."

"Or Emil," he said, as he put his hand on her stomach.

Christine smiled. She knew Jacob wanted a boy so badly; one who could take over the business someday... one he could play soccer with in the garden. She looked away and avoided him. At the last visit to the hospital, the doctor had told her it was a girl. She hadn't dared to tell him yet. It would simply devastate him. Now, she didn't know if she should keep it a secret until the baby was born. Maybe Jacob would change his mind once he saw his beautiful daughter. Maybe then he wouldn't care what gender it was anymore.

She had no idea how to break it to him.

Not now. Not today. Today is about finding a house. A new home for the family. It's not a day to worry.

"I love this house," she whispered. "It's just perfect."

"I know," he said. "It's everything we've been looking for."

They had been looking for a long time to find the right home for them to start their family... a home for their child to grow up in.

"Look, there are children playing in the street," Christine said. "That's perfect. I can take the ferry to the mainland every morning to go to the office, and you get to stay here and enjoy your life and take care of our boy. The harbor is only a few minutes away. I can even ride my bike there and take it with me on good days. Get some exercise. It's perfect. Oh, Christine, we're going to be very happy here. I can just feel it."

The real estate agent approached them. "So, I take it you like it?"

"We love it," Christine said. "We love the house, the garden with all its flowers. We love the street, the island, everything."

The real estate agent smiled even wider, probably at the prospect of making a lot of money, Christine thought. But she didn't care. Jacob's business made good money now, and it was time for them to live a little.

"It's ready to be moved into right away," she said. "It's been empty for quite a while. So, do you want to sleep on it or..."

Jacob looked at Christine, whose eyes were begging him.

I love this one. I love it. Let's just take it. Oh, please say we'll take it. Don't start talking about the price. Just take it.

"I say we finish the paperwork right away," he said. "We're ready to put in an offer."

EIGHTEEN

JULY 2014

It went wrong from the very beginning. Morten picked me up in his car at nine o'clock. He parked on the road, and I jumped in. I leaned over and kissed him. His kiss felt emotionless, slightly reluctant.

"Something wrong?" I asked.

Morten drove onto the road. He snapped at me. "No, nothing is wrong. Why would you say that? Why do you always assume something is wrong?"

"I don't know. You just don't seem very happy to see me," I said. The disappointment was eating at me. I had been looking forward to seeing him, and then he showed up angry. Wasn't he looking forward to this as much as I was? Maybe he was just worried about the meeting with the chief of police.

"I brought a little something for the trip," I said, and held up a thermos with coffee. "I also brought some of my home-made cake."

Morten hardly looked. His silence made me nervous. I grabbed a piece of the cake and ate it, hoping Morten wouldn't see me. He knew I was an emotional eater, and that I had gained a lot of weight over the last year, due to all the stress and emotional turbulence I had been through. He also knew I was trying to lose a couple of pounds and tried to support me. It was just so hard for me. Going through all the stress I was right now, I simply couldn't keep to a diet. Maybe I didn't really want to. Maybe I liked it like this. It had sort of become my thing. Eating made me happy.

"Do you want me to pour you some coffee?" I asked. "I brought cups."

"It's a little dangerous to pour hot coffee while we're driving," Morten said. "Wait till we're parked at the port waiting for the ferry."

I shrugged. "Okay."

Silence broke out between us. An awkward long silence.

What is wrong with him? Did I say something? Did I do something?

"So, did you have a nice evening with Jytte?" I asked.

Morten answered with a grumble.

"What was that?"

"Nothing." Morten exhaled. "She's giving me a hard time. That's all."

"A hard time? How's that?" I asked and stuck my hand into the bag and found another piece of cake.

"You don't want to know."

I bit my lip. I hated how he always excluded me when it came to his daughter. Anything else in his life, he would include me and tell me everything, even ask for my advice. Even when it came to his work. But, as soon as it was her, I had no business. It frustrated me. When you love someone, you want to be a part of every area of their life. Not just some of it. This was obviously bothering him enough to make him moody and ruin our trip. So, why couldn't I know what it was?

"Maybe I do," I mumbled, while looking out the window.

The port was coming up ahead of us. There were a lot of cars already waiting for the next ferry. The trip across to the mainland only took twelve minutes, and the ferry left three times an hour, so many of the people living on the island had jobs on the mainland and took the trip every morning to go to work.

"What was that?"

Morten drove into a lane and parked the car. I could see the ferry approaching in the distance. "I just said that maybe I would like to know what it was that Jytte was giving you such a hard time about."

Morten rubbed his chin. He had shaved this morning and was even wearing a tie. Maybe this meeting was more important than I had first thought. Was he worried about losing his job if they decided on the cutbacks? Was he keeping his worries from me?

"I don't want to bother you with what we're dealing with. Besides, Jytte would kill me if I did. She already thinks I'm sharing too much with you. She made me promise that what I talked about with her would stay between us. Guess she is afraid of losing her father, the poor thing.

The poor thing? More like poor manipulating thing!

I grabbed a bigger piece of the cake and ate it in order to keep quiet and not say anything that I would later regret. I couldn't believe that girl. She was deliberately keeping me out in the cold, wasn't she?

I swallowed my anger, along with the chocolate cake, and washed it down with coffee. I didn't speak for a little while.

"Now, I would like some of that coffee," Morten said.

I poured him a cup and handed it to him.

"Oh, by the way," he said, as he swallowed the first sip. "It looks like I'm going to have to cancel our dinner plans for Friday night."

"This Friday? But we were going to go out for the first time in weeks. Why do you have to cancel?"

"Jytte is having her birthday party at the club, remember? I rented the place for her."

My eyes grew big and wide. "But, you told me she said she didn't want any adults there." My voice was shaking. A lump grew in my throat. Jytte's birthday was two weeks ago, and I had given her the most beautiful bracelet. She, in return, had declared that I wasn't coming to her party, but up until now, Morten had told me that neither was he. He told me it was her being a teenager and not wanting adults to ruin her party.

The ferry was now in the port and being emptied of the few cars that drove onshore. The cars in front of us turned on their engines and started to drive onboard. Morten followed.

"I guess she had a change of heart," Morten said.

We drove onto the ferry and parked behind an RV... probably German tourists going back home. Fanoe island was always packed with German tourists at this time of year.

"A change of heart? I can't believe her," I said, startled.

"Oh, come on, Emma. She's a teenager. You know how they can be sometimes. Don't take it personally."

Personally? How can I not take this personally? I'm the only one she hasn't invited to this thing. It is personal. It doesn't get any more personal that this! Can't you see it? Why are you not upset about this? Why don't you tell her you want me there too? Why don't you tell her that I'm a big part of your life now, and that she has to accept that and treat me right? I'm not asking for much here. I really don't think I am.

Morten sipped some more coffee while the ferry started moving. Some people went outside to look around while we were sailing. I used to love watching the island disappear and breathing in the breeze, but not today. Today, Morten and I stayed in the car. I kept stuffing myself with the cake, in order to not say anything I would later regret, while Morten drank his coffee. I felt like steam was pouring out of my ears. I was furious. And hurt. Mostly hurt, I guess. I had tried so hard to get this girl to like me, and still, she just kept ignoring me and pretending that I didn't exist.

The worst part was that Morten let her.

NINETEEN

JULY 2014

Jesper Melander could hardly contain his excitement anymore. He was looking through the newspapers online and couldn't believe how far this had reached. All of the big newspapers had written the story, his story.

Finally, it had begun. Everything was going as planned. The island was in shock at the brutality of this killing, they wrote. He liked that word shock. It had such a wonderful ring to it, especially when you said it out loud. And it described precisely the state he wanted the other islanders to be in. That paralyzed state when they are unable to act. Oh, how he loved it. And the best part was that he had only just begun. The beauty of his plan was comprehensive. It was brilliant.

"Shock, shock, shock, people are in shock, it is shocking..." he said with a grin, while scrolling through the articles. Jesper hadn't expected to feel this thrilled about executing his plan. But, somehow, it had made him feel alive, made him feel like his life finally had a purpose.

He was a man on a mission. Like Dorothy. She was on a mission too. Jesper started humming, and soon he was singing the songs from *The Wizard of Oz*.

A second later, he was dancing on the floor. He grabbed the listing of the house on Niels Sørensens Vej that he had printed out from the internet. He knew they would love the house. Finally, they had decided on one. He had watched them as they looked at houses all over the island for weeks. Finally, it was closing time. And they moved fast, he was thrilled to discover. Before noon, they had put in an offer. Now, all he had to do was wait. The sellers would surely accept the offer, wouldn't they? Of course they would. The house had been vacant for quite a while. It was a lot sooner than Jesper had expected to be able to strike again, but that was only to his advantage.

The sooner the better.

Jesper thought back to the faces of the couple he had surprised in bed... the gorgeous sight of the red blood spreading on the sheets... the screams of the wife... the crunchy sound of the knife going through the flesh. Oh, and that look the wife had given. Those wide fearful eyes.

It was better than sex. He sang out loud again.

Then he burst into laughter. He couldn't wait to see that same look on the new couple's faces. What were their names again?

Jesper searched in his notes. Ah, yes. There they were. Jacob and Christine Hansen.

What wonderfully ordinary names. Mr. and Mrs. Denmark.

They were so ordinary, it almost hurt. They would go on to live boring meaningless ordinary lives, wouldn't they? No one would ever know about them. They would never do anything extraordinary, anything spectacular. No one in this forsaken country ever did. It was the country of mediocrity. Being ordinary was celebrated, encouraged even.

What a waste of life.

Well, now that was about to change. At least for this couple. The press would be all over the news in just a matter of days.

Once he was done with them, their names would be forever burned into the minds of the Danish people.

TWENTY
MAY 2009

Louise was shown inside a small room and asked to wait. She found a chair. It was quite uncomfortable. Maybe it was just her being edgy and wondering if she was making a mistake by coming here.

He had sent her a letter inviting her to come. Then, she had applied for permission to visit, and a week later, they had granted it. All she had to do was to show up with this letter and personal ID, it stated. And then they had sent her a list of things she couldn't bring.

She had to put all her stuff in a locker at the security entrance, and then walk through a metal detector. She had brought a cake. She wasn't the type to bake, so she had bought it at the bakery.

She was allowed to bring food, it had said in the letter. She just had to be aware that they might search it for drugs or other illegal items. And, it had to go through a scanner, so they could see if she was hiding something in it.

She wasn't. It was just an ordinary carrot cake. He had told her he liked carrot cake, and that he missed eating carrot cake. So she decided to take one to him. That would give them something to do while visiting, in case they ran out of subjects to talk about. Louise feared that awkward silence more than anything. It always made her feel so insecure. She never knew where to put her hands when she was insecure.

She put the cake on the small wooden table in front of her. There was a gray bench against the wall. It was as long as a bed and was padded. Louise wondered if that was for when a prisoner had many visitors, because it could fit a lot of people, but in the letter they had told her there could be no more than three visitors at the same time.

The door opened and Louise gasped. Two officers, or guards, or whatever they were called, escorted Bjarke inside. Louise rose to her feet. The door closed behind him, and the guards disappeared. They were alone.

Louise's heart was pounding in her chest. There he was. Right in front of her stood Bjarke Lund. The man she had watched over and over again on her TV screen. The man the entire world outside of these thick walls called dangerous.

He was looking at her. It made her nervous. Then, he smiled. "Finally, we meet," he said.

Her eyes met his. They were even deeper brown that she thought. She had always loved a man with brown eyes. He looked at her like he wanted to eat her alive. It made her feel special. This was the man everyone was talking about. Here he was. Here he was with her. Not with some beautiful tall model or actor, no, with her. With Louise.

His hungry look made her giggle.

"I've brought cake," she said.

"I thought I smelled something good."

Louise laughed awkwardly. "You want some?"

"Sure do."

They sat at the table. Louise broke off a piece of the cake with her fingers and handed it to him. He took a big bite and closed his eyes.

"Oh my. I had forgotten how delicious carrot cake is. Oh. It's wonderful. Thank you so much for bringing this. You're my saving angel, aren't you?"

Louise giggled again. "You told me you missed eating carrot cake, remember?"

Bjarke nodded with a smile. "I do remember that. Guess I'm just not used to people listening to what I have to say."

His face turned serious. Louise knew why. It was so unfair that they didn't listen to him. He had told her over and over again how they had judged him beforehand, because of the story with his mother, and there was nothing he could do to change their opinion of him. He was falsely convicted, and there was not a damn thing he could do about it. He had to accept the facts.

It's all about making the best of what life hands you, he wrote in one of his letters.

Louise didn't agree. She thought he should fight for his freedom. But he had told her when they spoke on the phone that it was no use.

"Unless they can find someone else to blame for this, unless someone else confesses to have done this, and they can prove it, then I'm pretty much stuck here."

Now, sitting in front of him in this small room, Louise wanted so badly to do just that. She wanted to help him get out.

Once he was done with his cake, Bjarke grabbed her leg under the table and pulled her closer. Louise shrieked. He put his face close to hers. She could smell his breath. She could feel his beard against her skin. She breathed hard.

"My, you're beautiful," he whispered. "There are so many things I want to do to you."

He stared at her intensely, while his hand climbed up under her skirt and touched her panties. "I dream about you every night, Louise. I have to have you. I have to taste you."

Louise gasped for breath. Never had a man spoken to her in

this way before. To her surprise, she realized she liked it. She enjoyed every word, and what it made her feel.

"I dream about you too," she managed to say.

"I want to take you on that bench right now," he said. "We're allowed to have sex with visiting girlfriends."

Louise really liked that he called her his girlfriend. No one had ever wanted her like this before. "But... but Bjarke... I've... I've never..."

"It would be an honor to be your first," he said.

Bjarke Lund didn't wait for her answer. He lifted her up and threw her onto the bench. With a wicked grin, he held her down and made a woman of her.

TWENTY-ONE

JULY 2014

"Yeah, just as I suspected, we're not getting any help with this case from the mainland."

Morten came out from the red brick police station and jumped inside of the car where I had been waiting, writing some ideas down on the laptop.

By the time he came out of the meeting, I had almost finished the cake.

"What?" I said. "But what do they expect? That you do it all alone?"

"The chief said that we're supposed to be able to deal with these kinds of things on our own. A double homicide doesn't require an entire team to solve. That's what he said."

"Well, did you tell him that there are only four officers on the entire island? Four officers to cover two cities and a load of tourists who want to feel safe. Did you say it was going to be impossible for you to solve this on your own?"

Morten looked at me angrily. "What do you take me for? Of course I told him that. But his hands are tied, he said. There isn't anything he can do. Plus they're considering cutting us down to two officers. They'll decide this fall."

"The press is going to be all over this as soon as the families find out. I mean, they want to know who did this. They want him behind bars. We all do."

Morten sighed. "Don't you think I know that? Can't you just leave it alone? This is my problem, not yours."

I scoffed. "Wow. And here I thought we were in this together. I thought we were a part of each other's lives."

"Well, I need to have at least some privacy," Morten said. "If I am to keep being me, and not just be a clone of you, then I need to have some space, to have my own life as well. You're kind of smothering me, and I'm losing myself and who I am here."

Morten turned on the engine. I stared at him, completely baffled.

What the hell was going on here?

"You're losing yourself? I'm smothering you?" I said.

Morten lifted his hands, annoyed, in the air. He made an irritated growl. "It's like you're swallowing me here, Emma. Like, for every day that passes, I'm losing myself. I have stopped living my own life and started living yours instead. All the things I used to do, I never do them anymore."

I had no idea what to say. Those words coming out of him sounded nothing like him. He had never said anything about these things before. Why now, all of a sudden?

Jytte. It has to be coming from her.

It all made sense now. Of course it came from her. She had been giving him a hard time all night last night, telling him that he had changed, that he never did the things he used to, that he was losing himself, that he was living my life instead of his own, and so on.

Was she really that crafty?

I really didn't like to think so. I really wanted her to be this innocent young girl who just missed her father, but lately, there had been a few too many examples of her trying to get between us.

The question was what would Morten do about it? Would he choose her over me?

"I'm sorry, Emma," he said, and looked at me. "It's just all the pressure right now. I had to talk to the parents yesterday, and to be frank, it was awful. Luckily, I wasn't the one to tell them the news, as the local police did that, but I spoke on the phone with them afterward, and they were just so devastated. They didn't understand how this could happen to their son. I... I... it broke my heart, Emma. And now this? What do I tell them when they call me to ask how the investigation is going? I gave them my phone number. I told them they could call me day or night if they had any concerns or questions. Once the first week has passed, they'll start wondering when the killer is going to be caught. What do I tell them? That it might take months to get to the bottom of this, because I'm the only one on the case? When do I tell them that?"

I put a hand on Morten's shoulder to try to make him relax. He was very tense.

"Let's just go," I said. "Let's go talk to this guy who threatened Jonas Boegh."

I had found the IP address that the email was sent from, and knew that Furious's real name was Poul Beckman. He lived less than an hour's drive north of Esbjerg.

Morten was quiet most of the way. I tried to speak and cheer him up but had no luck.

While in the car, Morten's phone suddenly rang, and he found a rest area to pull off at, so he could speak. Morten always followed the rules so neatly. Even though it was illegal to speak on the phone while driving, I always did it anyway.

I looked at him while he walked around in the parking lot and talked.

His face was very serious. It frightened me slightly.

Once he was done, he stood for a few seconds outside the car, like he needed to catch his breath before he got back in. He was pale.

"Who was that?"

"Forensics. They wanted to give me a preliminary report."

"So, what did they say?" I asked. His pale face made me fear what would come next.

Morten looked at me. He looked like he was about to throw up.

"You're scaring me here, Morten. What is it?"

"He took his heart," he whispered.

"He did what?"

"The man's heart is missing. It was cut out. Removed." He sighed. "That's why there was so much blood. The guy was still alive when it was done. Probably unconscious, but still."

"Why the heck would someone take another person's heart? A souvenir?" I said, feeling slightly nauseated myself. This thing sounded less and less like an assassination over money.

"I... I don't know. I'm no expert..." Morten threw his hands in the air. "Maybe like a hunter taking the heart of its prey."

"Like a trophy?"

Morten shook his head. He turned the key and started the car again. "I don't know."

"But now you have something you can use when interrogating Poul Beckman. This hasn't been in the newspapers yet, so if he knows anything about it, then he knows a little too much."

"Good point."

Morten steered the car back onto the road, and we continued toward Tarm, the city whose name meant gut in English, which I had always found to be strange... that anyone would name a city that.

Even if I was disgusted by the news, I did feel a little better. Finally, Morten and I were communicating again. We were talking and working together. I liked that.

"Anything else they could tell you?" I asked after a little while. "Any fingerprints, shoeprints, fibers, hairs?"

"Nothing. He was very careful."

"A pro."

Morten shrugged. "Or at least intelligent."

"That too."

"What about the shoes?" I asked.

"What about them?" Morten asked.

"They're not your everyday shoes. Why don't you try to track them? Where do you buy shoes like those?"

Morten looked at me and laughed.

"What?"

"Sometimes you're just such a girl. The shoes."

Morten took an exit and drove onto a small street, guided by his GPS. "What is that supposed to mean? Those kinds of shoes you can't buy in any ordinary shop, I'll tell you that much."

The GPS told us we had reached our destination. Morten parked in front of the house. We hadn't called in advance, because we didn't want this guy to run, so we had to take the chance that he would be home.

"Well, that might be. But I don't have time to call all the shoe shops in the area to find out where you can buy these. I would, if it wasn't just me on this case, but unfortunately, it is. Now, I'll go knock on the door to this house and hope to find this guy at home. You stay here."

"Go get him," I said with a smile. I grabbed my laptop from the back seat and put it on my knees. I found an unprotected Wi-Fi network from somewhere nearby and went online. "Don't forget this."

I reached across his seat and handed him the email. "Don't forget to find out how much he knows about a body's anatomy. Not everyone would know how to cut out a heart."

"I got this," Morten said, slightly offended, and grabbed the email. "Last time I checked, I was the police officer here."

"Okay. You're right. You're the man."

Morten leaned over and kissed my nose, then left the car. I pretended to be on the computer until I saw him walk inside the house. As soon as his back disappeared, I sprang out of the car and ran around the house. I wanted to see this guy in person. Luckily for me, he liked to leave the window open to the living room on such a warm summer day.

TWENTY-THREE

JULY 2014

"So, what can I do for you, officer?"

The voice had to be Poul Beckman's, I thought. I didn't dare to look in the window, in case either of them saw me. I felt ridiculous squatting underneath the window like this. But I was just so curious, I couldn't help it. I promised myself I wouldn't sit here for long. If Morten found me, he would think I had finally lost it.

"I'm sorry to disturb you like this, Mr. Beckman," Morten said. "But I'm here because of this email."

There was a silence and I suspected that Morten had handed Poul Beckman the printout. I would kill to be able to see his face right now, but I didn't dare to look.

"I... I'm sorry, officer. The email was written in anger. I... I never meant anything by it. A harmless joke."

Morten cleared his throat. "Well, not as harmless as you might think. I take it you haven't heard what happened to Jonas Boegh and his wife?"

Hadn't heard it? It was all over the news? If he pretended to not have heard it, he had to be lying.

"Heard what?"

"It's been on the news all day yesterday and this morning," Morten said.

"I'm sorry. I'm a lorry driver. I haven't been in the country the past week. Just got back from a trip to Poland this morning. I've been sleeping all day, because I had to drive all night."

"Do you have anyone who can confirm that?" Morten asked.

"Sure. My boss can tell you I was there. The company I delivered the goods to can as well. I can have them contact you, if you like."

"Probably going to need that."

"So, what happened to them?" Poul Beckman asked.

"They were murdered in their home while they were in their bed."

There was a pause. I wanted so badly to look up, but did I dare? I wanted to see if this guy was a liar or not. I lifted my head slowly and peeked inside. There he was... slightly over-weight, red beard, bald. He was shaking his head slowly while looking at the photograph Morten had shown him.

"I... I don't know what to say," he murmured. "I guess I can understand why you'd come to me... you know, after that email I sent."

"You did tell him to sleep with one eye open."

Poul Beckman sighed. "I was angry. I have issues with anger, okay? She was my daughter... he got the creep off. I was frustrated. Helpless. I let the anger get the best of me. What would you have done?"

"Probably not have written a threatening email," Morten said, with his calm voice.

"Okay, so I was mad at the guy. I get it. I have a motive. I might want to hurt him, but killing him? Killing him and his wife? Don't you think I would have chosen to kill the kid instead? To hurt the one who actually hurt my daughter?"

He made a good point. Didn't sound like he was lying

either. Either he was innocent, or a really good actor. Plus, he had an alibi.

He could have done it anyway. Who would notice if he made a stop on the way?

"Okay, Mr. Beckman. I'll leave you for now, but you should stay in the country, in case we need to talk to you again," Morten said.

"I can't do that. I drive a lorry!" Poul Beckman said, raising his voice. "It's my entire life. I need to make money. I have to pay alimony. My ex and her new husband insisted on putting my daughter in a boarding school, and I have to pay half of it. It's ruining me! If you ask me to stay in the country, I'll make no money!"

"I'm sorry, Mr. Beckman, but you'll have to stay here until I tell you otherwise. I can't have you suddenly disappearing on me."

"That's BS and you know it." Poul Beckman was yelling now.

Uh-oh.

I felt my heart rate go up, but Morten remained calm. He was very good in situations like this. "Mr. Beckman, you have to calm down, or I'll have to take you in. Do you hear me?"

I could hear Mr. Beckman snort aggressively. "Please, leave my house. I need to get some sleep," he said, growling.

I could hear them walking toward the door. I crawled along the house wall, hoping and praying I would make it to the car before Morten got out. I could hear them by the front door, and I stormed toward the car, opened the door and crept inside, then took my laptop back on my knees, just as I saw Morten walking toward me. I smiled and waved. He got inside and started the car.

I was out of breath but managed to hide it. I tapped on the computer. "So, how did it go?" I asked.

"Fine," he said with a grin.

"What?"

"Did you get those green marks on your knees while sitting in the car?"

I looked down and saw very visible grass stains made from crawling across the grass. Then I blushed.

Morten laughed and shook his head. "Is there any more chocolate cake left?"

TWENTY-FOUR

MAY 2009

Louise was smiling while putting on lipstick. She watched her face in the mirror. It had changed. She had changed. Ever since her visit to the prison, everything inside of her had changed. At first, she had been a little taken aback, a little scared when he had taken her like that in the visiting room, but after a little while, she had learned to enjoy it. He had been rough. His hands had hurt her, but she had kind of liked it. She had liked the way it made her feel.

Like a real woman.

For the first time in her thirty-eight years on this earth, she felt loved. For the first time, she felt like she was worth something. She had even cooked for once. She had made lasagna, and the smell was intoxicating. She was going to cook for herself from now on, and not just eat microwave dishes or her mom's food that she always stuffed in her freezer every time they came by. No, Louise had realized that she was actually capable of doing things herself, of taking care of herself. Bjarke Lund had taught her that. During her visit, after they had sex, they had talked. He had told her she could do anything she wanted to in life.

"Anything?" she said. "But... but I have a mental health condition," she said. No one had ever talked to her like he did... like she was an equal.

"So what?" he said. "Lots of people have mental health conditions, yet still do big things."

"Really?"

"Sure. Besides, I don't think you're so different. You seem pretty normal to me. Believe me, you can do a lot more than you give yourself credit for."

So, Louise had started doing things she had never dared before... and with great success. She was determined to be able to take care of herself and not depend so much on her parents anymore. Up until now, they had done everything for her. They had washed her clothes, they had cooked for her, and they even took care of her finances. But that was about to change. Louise wanted to take control of her own life. She had already done so by visiting Bjarke Lund without her parents knowing it. And she was going to visit him again, next week, and probably the week after that again.

Her parents noticed the change when they came to visit later that evening. As usual, her mother had brought a casserole, assuming that Louise had no food in the house.

"You look different," she said, as she air-kissed Louise's cheek. "Did you do something to your hair?" She gasped. "Are you wearing lipstick?"

Louise's dad smiled and held her tight when he hugged her. "You smell good," he said.

Louise smiled and closed the door behind them. "Come in."

"What's going on with you?" her mother asked. "I don't like this, Hans." She looked at Louise's dad.

"I think it's fine, Marlene," he whispered back. "She seems to be doing well. She looks happy."

"Get that lipstick off, honey. It looks hideous." Louise's mom reached out a hand and smeared the lipstick with her thumb. She held Louise's head hard with the other hand. Louise tried to protest, but it was always hard when it came to her mother. It was like she possessed this power over her, like she could make her into a small child with just a look or a word.

"Mom... please, don't."

"It won't come off," she said. Louise's mom then spat on her thumb and tried again.

Louise moaned in humiliation.

Her mom finally looked at her and smiled. "There. It's off. Looks much better like this."

Then she let go of Louise, who cried and pulled away.

"Oh, don't be such a baby," her mother said. "You look much prettier this way. You looked like a whore with that lipstick on. And you're not a whore, are you, Louise?"

Louise bent her head and shook it. "N-no."

Her mother patted her on the shoulder. "Good. I didn't think so. I didn't raise you to be one either. It's a good thing you have us to guide you. I know you're not well, honey. I know your condition makes you like this. That's why your mom and dad are here to help you. You don't know any better."

Louise's mom went into the kitchen and her dad followed a few steps behind. He didn't even look at Louise as he passed her, holding the casserole.

"Come on, let's get something to eat," Louise heard her mother chirp from the kitchen. "I'm starving. Oh, you cooked, did you? Well, that was very nice of you, dear, but we can't eat that. Let's have the casserole. At least we know what's in that, right?"

Louise sniffled, and then took a deep breath. She looked at herself in the mirror in the hallway. The change was gone. The light in her bright blue eyes that had been there since her visit to the prison was gone. In a matter of seconds, her mother had managed to slap her right back to where she came from. Louise stared at her smeared lipstick and touched her lips gently in the same way Bjarke Lund had done. She felt anger rise inside of her. She had often felt angry when her mother humiliated her, but never like this. Bjarke had talked to her about anger. He had told her that anger was good for you. It wasn't supposed to be bottled up inside of you. It was a healthy feeling. It had to come out somehow, or something inside of you would break.

His words had stirred up something inside of Louise, and she realized that years of bottled-up anger were about to erupt, and she wasn't sure she would be able to control it when it did.

She wasn't sure she wanted to.

TWENTY-FIVE

JULY 2014

It all went really fast. Once they put the offer in that afternoon, after visiting the house, the real estate agent called that night and told them that the owner had accepted. Now, all that was left was the paperwork.

In two days, it was all done, and they signed the papers. Friday, they were handed the keys, and started to move in. It was the fastest closing this real estate agent could remember, she told them, as she shook hands goodbye.

It suited Christine perfectly that it had gone so fast, because she was ready to start decorating and wanted it done while she still had the energy and strength. Once her stomach got bigger, she knew it would be too hard.

Jacob smiled and kissed her cheek as he moved a box into the kitchen. "I can't believe this is actually ours. Finally, our own house," she said.

They had been looking for what felt like ages for the right house, and she had been on the verge of giving up... until Jacob asked if she wanted to go live on Fanoe island. His offices were in Esbjerg, so they might as well live out there as in some house north of the city. As soon as they started looking on Fanoe,

Christine knew they were in the right place. She just felt it. It was so perfect for her. Especially now that she was about to become a mother.

"Emil is going to love it here," Jacob said, as he carried another box inside.

Christine had wanted to move the kitchen in first, as they were going to need that the most. That, and a bed to sleep in, naturally. He was going to get that next. Jacob had wanted to stay in their rented house a couple of nights more, because they had it until the end of the month, but Christine was so excited about the new house that she wanted to sleep there from the first night.

"Sure... he will," she said.

She watched Jacob as he carried the heavy box inside the kitchen. They were so happy at this moment. It was like nothing could come between them.

But you're deceiving him. You have to tell him at some point. You can't keep it a secret forever.

Christine sighed. No, not now. Not today. She didn't want to ruin their happiness and joy right now. Maybe tomorrow. Or sometime next week when they were all settled in. Jacob had enough on his plate right now. The old house needed to be fixed up before they handed back the keys, and he didn't want Christine to lift a finger. He would let her unpack a few boxes, but other than that, he had told her to relax and just focus on *growing our little Emil*.

How could she break his heart and let him know? Would he be angry? Would he resent the baby? Would he resent her for it?

"There. That should be all the boxes for the kitchen," he said with a wide smile, as he came back into the living room where Christine was sitting on a chair that Jacob had moved in as the first thing, so she wouldn't have to stand up. Her legs had been quite swollen lately.

"Amazing," she said and got up. "Let me start unpacking."

"Now, remember to take breaks, darling. And don't forget to eat. Emil needs to grow, remember?"

Christine exhaled with a soft smile. "Of course."

"The movers will be here later. I have to go to the office for a few hours, then I'll be back, but you can tell them where to put our furniture, right? Just don't lift anything. Promise me that?"

Christine chuckled. Jacob had been so sweet and protective ever since she announced the pregnancy.

"I'll be fine. Just go."

"Are you sure? I have a meeting, but I could reschedule if you need me to," he said.

"There's no need for that. I'm fine here. I'm more than fine. I love this house. I love spending time here. I can't wait to get everything into place. I feel so good about this house. I feel so safe here."

Jacob smiled gently. Then he leaned over and kissed her. He opened the front door and stepped outside. Then he turned and looked at his wife again.

"I'm glad you like it. It's going to be a wonderful life for us here. Just you, me, and Emil. I can just feel how perfect it's going to be."

Sitting in his car on the street, watching Christine kiss her husband goodbye in the doorway, Jesper Melander couldn't agree more.

"It is going to be perfect," he whispered.

TWENTY-SIX

JULY 2014

The newspapers were all over the story about the angry father in the days after our visit to his house. They still were on it the following Friday morning when I sat in my kitchen going through the headlines.

The story about Jonas Boegh, who defended a rapist and set him free, seemed to be their favorite. Their next favorite was the story about the father allegedly avenging the daughter by killing Jonas. They were all theories, of course, but all the articles stated that the police were seriously looking into the matter. I had no idea how they knew about Poul Beckman. Neither did Morten, and it annoyed him immensely. He had been in a bad mood for days now, and I was getting a little annoyed with him. Especially the night before when he came to dinner. Once the kids finished eating, I started asking about the investigation.

"What about the shoes?" I asked. "Has anyone looked into that?"

"Enough with those shoes. What is it with you and the shoes?" he snapped at me.

It was unusual for me to hear him talk in a tone like that. He was always so calm and gentle.

"I just think it might be a good clue, that's all. If you can find where the killer bought them, then maybe the salesperson can describe him or even tell you who he is."

"It's a pair of shoes," Morten said. "There are a lot of shoe shops in this country. Do you seriously suggest that I contact all of them and ask about the shoes? I'm sorry. But I don't have time for that. It has been mentioned in all the newspapers, and on TV, and that has to do for now."

I sensed that he wanted me to leave it alone, so I did. I couldn't stop thinking about Poul Beckman and his bad temper. I had been digging a little into his background and knew he had been arrested more than once in bar fights, and he had once beaten his ex-wife's new husband with a baseball bat. I had my serious doubts about his alibi as well. It was a little too easy, I thought, and kept arguing with Morten about it.

"He could have done it anyway," I said.

"That might be," Morten argued. "But I have to stay with the facts, and there is nothing linking him to the killings. No blood, no DNA, no fingerprints, not even a shoeprint. Nothing places him at the scene of crime. Plus, his boss tells me he was on the road at the time of the killings."

"But he has a very good motive," I grunted.

"He does. But he is right. It doesn't make sense to kill the lawyer. He would have killed the boy instead."

I shrugged. It was a good point, but it had been his point and maybe just a clever excuse. "Maybe he's next? Maybe he's just waiting for everything to calm down a little, and then he can go after the kid. Get them both while he's at it."

Morten didn't want to discuss it anymore, so I left it alone. The atmosphere after that was tense and bad. We hardly spoke for the rest of the dinner, and afterward, Morten left, telling me he had promised to go home to Jytte right after work.

My guess was that he didn't tell her he came here to dinner.

Probably so he wouldn't have to argue with her about it. It was getting more and more ridiculous.

As I sat in my kitchen Friday morning and enjoyed my morning coffee, Sophia stopped by, and we talked for an hour or so. I told her about my troubles with Morten. It felt good to get it off my chest. I needed to talk to someone about it.

"I'm sorry, sweetie," she said. "Stepchildren can be so much trouble. I went through that same thing with a guy I dated. He was obsessed with keeping her happy, and she did not like me, so needless to say, we had to split up."

I stared at her. I really didn't want to have to split up. I hadn't really thought it would go that far, but now I was starting to.

"I'm sorry, sweetie," she said. "I'm sure you will figure it out. I mean, come on. It's Morten and Emma, right? They always figure things out."

"I hope so. I really do. Tonight he's going to Jytte's birthday party, and I'm not invited."

"That's rough," Sophia said.

I exhaled and finished my cup. Maya came into the kitchen and grabbed a cup. She had started drinking coffee when the amnesia thing happened. I felt sad as I watched her drink it. Everything was changing, and I wasn't sure I liked it. I wanted to go back to the way it used to be. I wanted everybody to go back to who they used to be.

TWENTY-SEVEN

"Welcome to the neighborhood!"

Jesper Melander could hardly hide his excitement. He was smiling from ear to ear as he lifted up the gift basket he had wrapped himself before coming to the house.

The woman he knew was called Christine looked at him, startled.

Her husband stood right behind her in the doorway.

"Who are you?" the man asked, pushing himself in front of her.

"I wanted to welcome you to the neighborhood by giving you this basket. Sorry, I'm Jesper."

Jacob shook his hand reluctantly. "Haven't I seen you somewhere before?"

"Well, I don't know," Jesper said with a grin. He was wearing black sunglasses, even though it was dark. He could tell how it confused them that they were not able to see his eyes.

"It's a little late," Jacob said, looking at his watch. "It's almost ten o'clock."

"Ah, come on," Jesper said. He walked closer to the door,

still grinning. "Never too late for a nightcap with your new neighbor, is it?"

They looked at each other. Jesper took off the glasses. It helped. Made them feel safer. "I brought you some rum. It's from Guatemala. Supposed to be the best in the world, they say."

"Well, that is awfully nice of you," Jacob said. "I guess we could have a glass. It is, after all, Friday."

Jacob stepped away from the door and let Jesper inside. "Christine, you know where everything is. Could you find us some glasses?"

"Sure," she said, and walked to the kitchen.

Jesper studied her every move. "Quite a beauty you've got yourself there, huh? Lucky guy."

Jacob relaxed further. Flattery always made people feel more comfortable.

"So, a brand-new house, huh? I love new houses. It's like a clean slate, right? Start all over. The beginning of something new and wonderful."

Christine returned, carrying two glasses. She put them down with an insecure smile. "Thank you," Jesper said. "You're not having anything?"

She shook her head shyly. "No," she said, and touched her belly without realizing it.

"Ah, I see," Jesper said.

"I'm going to bed; I'm tired," Christine said.

"Good night, sweetheart. I'll be up in little while."

"No need to hurry. We don't want to offend our new neighbor. Good neighbors are hard to find," she said, and kissed him gently on the cheek before she turned around and disappeared.

Jesper stared after her. He felt thrilled. He could hardly believe his luck. The woman was pregnant. They didn't come any more beautiful and innocent than that. He couldn't have planned it better himself. Oh, the beauty of this. He could hardly restrain himself.

His heart was beating fast and he was breathing heavily, as he pulled out the bottle of rum from the basket and opened it.

"Then, I guess it's just for the two of us," he said, and started pouring. He lifted his glass. "To good neighbors," he said, and they toasted.

"To good neighbors," Jacob answered.

"Ah. That's good stuff, huh?" Jesper said, after having emptied his glass.

Jacob had only sipped a little bit of his.

Jesper laughed.

"What's so funny?" Jacob asked.

"Oh, nothing. It's just that... well, I can't wait till I see your face once you realize what else is in the basket. It's just such a THRILL to meet new people, isn't it?"

Jacob looked confused. He looked at the basket. Then he smiled. "Oh, there's chocolate in there too?"

"YES!"

Jesper yelled so loud it made Jacob jump in his chair.

"But, there's more... something I can't wait to give that beautiful wife of yours. Something she can wear."

Jacob looked baffled, then looked inside of the basket again. He pulled out a pair of ruby red slippers.

"What is this?" he asked.

At first, he smiled, but seconds later, Jesper watched as his facial expression changed drastically, probably when he remembered the shoes being mentioned in the news as being found on one of the recent murder victim's bodies.

Jacob stared at Jesper with terror in his eyes, then threw the shoes on the floor. "What kind of a sick joke is this?" he asked, as he rose to his feet.

"Oh, it's no joke," Jesper said with a light laugh. "It's not funny at all."

"I think I have to ask you to leave my house immediately," Jacob said.

Jesper tilted his head. "Now, tell me, dearie, how can you talk if you don't have a brain?"

Jacob shook his head. "What are you talking about? Are you asking me a riddle? I think you're mad. Please leave."

Jesper didn't laugh again. He reached into his pocket and pulled out a knife, then walked quickly toward Jacob. Jesper spotted a flicker of horror in the man's eyes. Jacob tried to cover himself.

"Please, don't hurt me," he begged.

Jesper smiled and stroked his cheek. Oh, how he enjoyed these seconds. Those fragile rare seconds when his victims knew it was over, when they realized there was nothing they could say or do. He enjoyed the terror in their eyes while they searched for a way out, for a way to escape this certain fate of death. Jesper brought the knife to his throat, then sliced it with a satisfied groan.

While the blood rushed out of Jacob's throat onto the floor, Jesper held him against the wall, looking into his eyes, watching as the life was sucked out of him. Just before he let him fall to the ground, he whispered into his ear, "I don't know either... but some people without brains do an awful lot of talking... don't they?"

TWENTY-EIGHT

JULY 2014

Sophia had her mom stay with the kids and spent Friday evening at my house. We drank some wine and played cards, something we had started doing recently and enjoyed a lot. Jack came over as well and joined us for a card game of whist.

What I had thought would be a terrible evening turned out to be quite nice. The three of us had fun. After two bottles of red wine and a couple of stronger drinks, we were getting quite drunk, especially me. I guess I just wanted to forget about my troubles with Morten and the fact that he was at that birthday party, and I wasn't invited.

"Why the heck didn't he just tell that daughter of his that she had to invite you as well?" Sophia asked.

"I don't know," I said and took up a card.

"Well, I think he should have. Don't you, Jack?"

Jack had kept very quiet when discussing Morten and me. His eyes met mine. I really wanted to hear his opinion.

"I... I... I d-d-don't know," he said.

I took a sip of my gin and tonic. Of course, he didn't want to say anything bad about Morten. Jack never talked bad about anyone.

"But... I do know... that y-y-you d-deserve to be appreciated."

"Aw, that's such a sweet thing to say, Jack," Sophia said. "He's just such a sweetheart, isn't he?"

I bit my lip and nodded. Jack was looking at me intensely. I had always liked him. A lot.

"You're up, Emma," Sophia said.

My eyes left Jack's, and I took another card from the stack. I hardly looked at it. I couldn't escape this strange feeling. I looked up and my eyes locked with Jack's. It was very intense. My heart was beating hard.

"Hello? Earth to Emma," Sophia said. "It's your move."

"Oh, I'm sorry," I said, and looked down at my cards again. I put a card down and emptied my glass.

Jack poured me another drink. Our legs touched under the table.

What am I doing?!

I sipped my drink. My head was spinning. I wondered about Morten and how his night was. He was probably out having a lot of fun with his daughter. I couldn't believe how she had managed to come between us over the last several weeks. The way she had managed to keep him away from me was so frustrating. And there wasn't anything I could do about it. The more I tried to discuss it with Morten, the further he moved away from me.

I looked at the clock on my cooker. It was almost midnight. I had told Morten he could stop by and sleep here if he wanted to. He probably wasn't coming. I looked at my phone as well, to see if he had called or at least texted me good night. But there was nothing. Sophia put her hand on my shoulder.

"Forget him," she said. "If he really wants you, then no one can keep him from you. Not even his daughter."

"But, what if he doesn't want me enough?" I could hear my voice getting thick. I didn't want to cry, but it was hard not to. I felt so sorry for myself. With everything I was going through with the kids, now I had to have trouble with him as well. I really didn't need it. I really couldn't take anymore. Maybe it was just the alcohol. Maybe I was just too tired. This week had been exhausting. Plus, it annoyed me that I hadn't been able to get as much done on my next book as I wanted to. My editor was waiting for me to make the last corrections, but I couldn't really get to it properly. An hour here and there didn't amount to much. It was going to help when the kids went back to school. That was certain. But I really just wanted to have it done, so I could publish it and move on with my life.

Between that and the homicide next door and the trouble with my kids and boyfriend, I was ready to throw in the towel. It was just a little too much.

"I think I might need to go to bed," I said, and threw down my cards. Just as I spoke the words, the kitchen door opened, and Victor walked inside. He looked at me without blinking.

"Victor, what are you doing...?"

But Victor didn't hear me. He didn't even look at me. With a terrified look on his face, he started chanting.

TWENTY-NINE

JULY 2014

"Victor, stop yelling. Please, just stop!"

But, Victor didn't stop. He kept screaming at me like he wanted me to do something.

I grabbed his shoulders. "Stop it, Victor. Just look at me. You're dreaming."

"He must be sleepwalking," Sophia said. "My kids do that all the time. Be gentle. Don't scare him, Emma. It can be quite a shock for a sleepwalker to be woken up."

I tried to calm myself down, but Victor's screaming terrified me. "Please, sweetie, just stop screaming. It's all right. Mommy is here."

The door to the kitchen opened again, and Maya walked in. "What's going on?" she asked. "I heard someone scream."

"It's nothing, sweetie. Victor is just having a nightmare and won't wake up."

Victor was now covering his ears and bending forward while yelling.

"Calm down, sweetie. Please, just calm down." I tried to hug him, but he pulled away from me.

"I know that," Maya said.

"What was that?" I asked.

Maya walked closer to her brother. "What he's saying. I know it. It's from the film again."

I gasped. "*The Wizard of Oz?*"

"Oh, yeah. That's right," Sophia said. "It's what the Cowardly Lion says, you know the one without courage."

I looked at Victor, and suddenly, I was extremely sober.

"What's wrong?" Sophia asked. "You look like you saw a ghost."

I shook my head. "I don't know... it's just that... the last time Victor quoted something from that film, our neighbors turned up dead."

Sophia and Jack looked at each other.

"It's probably just a coincidence," Sophia said.

She didn't sound convincing. Just as abruptly as he had started screaming, Victor suddenly stopped. His eyes rolled back, and his body went soft. His legs collapsed under him, and I caught him just as he was about to fall. I picked him up in my arms and realized he was sound asleep.

"Let me get you back to bed," I whispered. "You too, Maya. You need your rest."

"I better get home as well," Jack said, and grabbed his jacket.

"Yeah, me too," Sophia said with a yawn. "I'll drop in tomorrow to make sure you're all right."

"Thank you for coming tonight, so I didn't have to be alone."

The two of them left and I carried Victor up the stairs. Maya followed me, after having locked the front door for me. Since the incident with the neighbors, I was being extra careful not to have any windows or doors left unlocked. Morten had told me the killer probably came in through a window in the basement, because they found it wide open. I wondered how a grown man could have gotten through those small windows, and figured we weren't dealing with a big guy.

I placed Victor in his bed and kissed him, wondering if he would sleep through the rest of the night. I walked out to Maya in the hallway. Knowing Victor was now safe and calm, I couldn't stop thinking about the killings again. Why would the killer take the victim's heart? Neither of the victims had been sexually abused, nor had anything in the house been stolen. The majority of killings had a sexual motive or had something to do with money. This seemed to have nothing to do with either.

What was it about then? Was it Poul Beckman's revenge for his daughter? But what was the idea of the red shoes then? Did his daughter wear red shoes? Did they maybe belong to her?

"I remembered something again," Maya said, as I walked her to her room. She crept under the covers, and I kissed her forehead. "I know, honey. I'm so happy you have finally started remembering things. I'm certain you will remember everything soon. Then, everything will be less scary for you."

"I remembered something else," she said. "Just before, when Victor was screaming, I remembered something else."

"What was that?"

"I remember asking one night you if you and dad were splitting up. I was a small child. Victor was just a baby. You had a huge fight."

I felt a knot in my stomach. I remembered something too from that time. I remembered the feeling. The sense that something was wrong, the terrifying feeling that it wasn't going to last, that we were breaking apart... the uncertainty.

Exactly the way I was feeling now about Morten and me. I exhaled deeply at the realization. "And what did I say?"

"You told me that was never going to happen."

THIRTY

JUNE 2009

It was the happiest day of her life. Louise knew all brides thought so on their wedding day, but she also knew that their happiness couldn't be measured against hers. Hers was special. It was more than normal.

She was ecstatic.

Finally, she was breaking out of her shell. Finally, she was no longer going to be her mother's little fragile girl, who couldn't do anything on her own, let alone make any decisions.

She had made one now. A big one. An irreversible one.

She twirled in the splendor of her wedding dress as she walked up the aisle of the prison chapel.

It wasn't her father walking by her side, giving her away. It was one of Bjarke's best friends, who had agreed to step up. Her parents had refused to come, and told her that if she married that monster, they would never speak to her again.

Even better, she had thought. *Another reason to do this.*

Not only was she marrying the man of her dreams, but she was also getting rid of her lifelong plague. It was what they called a win-win situation, wasn't it?

Bjarke was waiting for her next to the prison priest, smiling from ear to ear as well. The look in his eyes made Louise shed a tear of joy. He really loved her. He really did. She could tell. She had seen it in his eyes every Wednesday when she came to visit him, and she felt it on her body when he did all those things to her in the visiting room. She knew he loved her when he held her down and pressed that thing of his inside of her mouth. She knew he loved her when he almost choked her in an act of passion while making love to her... and when he played those games where she had to pretend she was someone else, like a young girl on her way home from school and he pretended to be raping her. She just knew it. He'd told her over and over again.

"You know, they say that you only hurt the one you love," he would whisper in her ear. And then he would do just that. He would hurt her. He'd bruise her badly in places the guards wouldn't see, and she would take it, let him, because it showed her how crazy he was about her, and she had never known love like that. He told her he knew what she liked. He knew she liked pain. And they were perfect for each other, because he liked to see people in pain.

He was so smart. Much smarter than Louise. And he had so much life experience. He knew everything. Louise felt so secure with him, and she couldn't wait to become his wife. And she was okay with only seeing him once a week for the next sixteen years.

What's the worst that can happen? she had asked herself after his proposal in the visiting room at the prison. *What if he's lying? What if he did kill those people?*

Well, at least he was in prison, right? Louise believed in his innocence, but she also knew she wasn't the brightest among girls. She figured that, even if he was lying, even if he was as bad as everyone tried to tell her he was, then at least he would be in prison. There was no way he could ever harm her. Not that he would ever want to. He loved her. It was different with her. He had told her that she was the first one he had ever loved.

It was perfectly safe.

Her parents had tried to stop the wedding from happening. They tried to disempower her with the argument that her mental health condition made her unstable and unable to make decisions on her own.

But they hadn't succeeded. They were still working on it, and therefore Bjarke and Louise had decided to move the wedding up. And now it was too late. Now, the priest was looking at Louise and waiting for her to say the most important words she would ever say in her life.

"I do."

The priest pronounced them husband and wife, and they kissed. The church was empty, except for Bjarke's friend, who now clapped.

It had been all over the newspapers that the notorious killer Bjarke Lund was getting married, and Louise had a hard time walking in the street without being attacked by journalists or people wanting to tell her how stupid she was for marrying him.

She didn't care. It was all worth it. Now, she was a married woman, and no one, other than Bjarke, could ever tell her what to do.

No one.

THIRTY-ONE

JULY 2014

"I don't understand why I have to see him when you tell me he's not even my real dad," Maya said over breakfast.

I was exhausted and didn't want to fight about this. It was a good sign that she was arguing; it was more like her, but I wasn't in the mood for this right now. I had slept awfully, tossing and turning and thinking about Morten and why he hadn't at least texted me. Didn't he care about me at all? Or was he angry with me? Today, I had arranged for my ex-husband to come and see his daughter. He was on a trip to a city close to us anyway, so he had called and asked if he could see his children. Maya wasn't his biological daughter, but I still wanted him in her life. He was the closest she came to having a father.

"Because he is your dad. Maybe not biologically, but for most of your years growing up, he was the only dad you had," I said, and finished my cup of coffee. It wasn't working today. The caffeine didn't seem to do the trick. Victor was looking forward to seeing his father again and had run upstairs to comb his hair to look good for him.

"But I hardly remember him. What about my real dad? Shouldn't I see him instead?" Maya argued.

A part of me enjoyed arguing with her again. I had missed that. It was good. Maybe she was, after all, improving.

"You don't know him," I said, and poured myself another cup in the hope that it would kick in at some point. It had to. I wasn't going through this entire day feeling like this.

"I don't know Michael either."

"Don't call him that. He's your father."

Maya exhaled. "I don't remember him. All I remember is the two of you fighting and me being scared that you were going to split up, which you promised me you wouldn't, and then you did anyway. I feel like you're letting me leave with a stranger."

I sat down again and closed my eyes while rubbing my forehead. "It's just a lunch, Maya. Your dad has driven all the way from Copenhagen to take you out for a lunch. Can't you at least give him that?"

"I guess."

"Then go up and get dressed. He'll be here in half an hour."

Maya rolled her eyes and got up. I hid a smile, but it was hard. I felt like cheering and laughing.

My daughter just rolled her eyes at me! She's back!

At least her strange emotionless stage was phasing out. I was thrilled about that. She was acting more like a teenager again. But she still only had two memories back in almost three months. At this rate, she certainly wasn't going to remember anything from school, and there were only three weeks left until the start of school. I was frustrated and very worried about how this was going to work out. I wondered if hiring a tutor would help, or if it would end up confusing her more.

I looked toward the ceiling. "I need help here! God, please help me out. I can't do this alone. Send help, would you?"

Michael arrived late. Fifteen minutes later than planned. He looked confused as he stepped out of the car. I was waiting with Victor in the front garden, where he had been standing with his little backpack on for at least twenty minutes. He had put his rocks in the backpack. He insisted on taking them, even if they were only going to be gone for a few hours.

"You're late," I grumbled.

"I know," he said. "The traffic was crazy getting off the ferry. What's going on downtown? The road leading behind the church was barricaded. I had to drive all the way around the city to get here."

I shrugged. "I don't know," I said. "There's a knitting festival going on, but that's not until next weekend. That usually draws a couple of thousand people here."

Michael chuckled. "A knitting festival? You sure you don't miss Copenhagen?"

"Not even a little bit." I looked at Victor. "He's been ready for a long time. Be good to him, will you? He's really missed having a father in his life."

"Well, I'm not the one who decided to move all the way out here," Michael said. "Kind of feels like you're trying to keep me away from my children."

"Now, wait a minute," I said. "You were the one who told me you couldn't handle the two of them, and especially Victor... that Victoria couldn't handle them. You told me you couldn't have them visiting. That was before we moved."

I heard a noise and turned. There was Maya. She was standing right behind me. I smiled awkwardly, afraid she had heard what I said.

"Hi, sweetie. You ready?"

I could tell by the look on her face that she had heard everything. She looked hurt. That she was showing emotions was good, but this wasn't the kind I was looking for. Her eyes were flickering from side to side, like she was suddenly remembering something.

"Victoria," she said.

"Yes. That's daddy's new wife. You remember her?" I asked.

"I lived with her," she said. Then she looked up at her

father. I could see such distrust in her eyes. "You... you... you hit her. And you hit me. That's why I decided to run away. That's why I stole the car. I wanted to get away. Where was I going?" Maya held a hand to her head.

I stared angrily at Michael. "What in... you hit her? You hit your wife? You hit Maya?"

Michael looked confused. "I... I'm sorry. I was stressed out that morning. The baby had kept me up all night. Victoria was on my case... nagging me about Maya, so I lost it... I know it's bad... Maya came in and started yelling at me that I couldn't treat my wife like that, so I... I'm sorry. It was just a slap."

Maya touched her cheek. Then she shook her head. "No, it wasn't. It was more than that. You used your fist. You hit both Victoria and me with a clenched fist," Maya said, and took a step backward.

I felt awful. Michael had more than once slapped me across the face, but he had never touched the children, and he had never done more than slap me... never with a clenched fist.

I grabbed Victor and pulled him back. Michael looked angry all of a sudden. I didn't feel comfortable.

"I think you should go, Michael," I said.

"Not without my children," he hissed. "I'm allowed to see my children. Come, Victor. Come with me. We're going to have fun today."

"Not today, Victor. Your dad is about to leave."

"For Christ sake, Emma. It's just a lunch. I've driven a long way to get here. Now, let me have my children before I get really mad."

"Not today, Michael. I'm sorry, kids, but I think we all need a break to think over our arrangement."

Michael walked closer. His face was turning red. "What the hell is that supposed to mean?"

"It means I need to know that you have your anger issues

under control before I let you be alone with your children again. That's what it means."

Michael growled, then reached out his hand and slapped me across the face. It hurt like crazy.

"Run, kids! Run into the house," I yelled.

Maya grabbed her brother and tried to drag him toward the house. I had no idea how much Victor understood the situation, but he wasn't moving. He stared at his sister's hands on his arm. Michael moved fast. Before I could react, he pushed Maya hard and caused her to fall backward with a scream, then he grabbed Victor's arm and dragged him toward the car.

"This one is mine, so I'm taking him," Michael said. "You'll never see him again. I promise you that much. I'll fight for my rights to him."

"Michael, don't do this. You have no idea how to handle him!" I yelled after them.

Victor started screaming.

"You know he doesn't like to be touched!" I said.

Michael forced the screaming Victor inside his car, and then slammed the door. "That's another thing," he said, walking angrily toward me with his fist in the air. I was afraid he would hit me again.

"You put all these ideas into his head that he is sick and can't be touched and all that. But it's nothing but nonsense. You're smothering him, making him sick with all your fussing. Now, I'm going to make my son into a man. I'll touch him if I want to, and I'll teach him to be a man."

"Michael. You don't know what you're doing. He was doing so well. You'll set him back with this. Please, don't take him from me!"

I was yelling at the top of my lungs, while pulling on the handle of the car. But it was locked. Michael smiled.

"You're never getting him back. I'll get the best lawyer in the world, and who do you think they'll give him to? The deranged lone mother who is a loose cannon and in a very unstable relationship, or the stable married couple with stable income and a stable life?"

I pushed Michael in anger. "Give him back to me. Now!"

Michael pushed me back. I fell to the ground and hurt my back. I was crying heavily now.

Please don't let this happen. Dear God. Please don't!

I felt desperate. Michael walked closer and bent over me, his clenched fist lifted into the air ready to hit me. I could hear Maya screaming behind me and raised my hands to protect my face. I closed my eyes and screamed, when suddenly, a voice cut through the air.

"Step away from the woman."

"What the hell...?" Michael said, then turned.

I looked up and saw Sophia. She was holding a gun in her hands. She was shaking like crazy. Behind her stood Jack.

"Y... you heard her. G... g... get away from Emma."

Michael scoffed and put his hands in the air. "I don't know who you think you are, but I'm the victim here. I just came here to be with my kids, and she's trying to keep me away from my own children."

"It's funny how she's on the ground with bruises on her face when you're the victim," Sophia said. "I know your type. I used to date them. Save your smart remarks for court. Release the kid," Sophia said, and pointed at the car. "Let Victor out."

"You've got to be kidding me," Michael said, chuckling. "Are these your friends? Are these the kind of people you're hanging out with? Scarecrow and Tin Man here? Two village idiots?"

"She told you to release the kid." Jack was remarkably clear when he spoke. His voice didn't even shake. "Do it!"

Sophia moved toward him like she was going to actually shoot him. She was really angry. I had never seen her quite like this. Michael was taken aback. He looked scared.

"Okay. Okay. Easy with the gun," he said. He found the car key and opened the door. Victor jumped out and ran toward me. He threw himself in my arms. I cried inconsolably and held him tight. My little boy, who never wanted me to touch him... suddenly, he wouldn't let go of me.

"This is not over, Emma," Michael yelled, as he got back into his car. "Believe me!"

I held Victor close while Michael spun the wheels down the street and disappeared. Maya ran to me and her brother and hugged us, and soon Jack and Sophia joined in. I was sobbing heavily and thanking them.

"And you always said that me having a gun in the house was a bad idea, huh?" Sophia said, with tears in her eyes. "Guess you won't say that again."

"Guess not," I said, and held all my little family tight.

I served coffee and freshly baked buns for everyone as soon as we came inside. I made hot chocolate for Victor and Maya, who both were shaken badly by this incident. Neither of them spoke a word. Victor seemed to shake it first. He ate his bun, then got up and said he would go play in the garden. Then he grabbed his bag of stones that he had collected at the beach and left us. My mind was spinning with all of this, and I couldn't wrap my head around it.

I should have seen it coming. I should have known somehow.

I couldn't believe I didn't realize what Michael was capable of. I had been married to the guy for ten years. I knew he had anger issues. He could sometimes yell at me for hours. He was a perfectionistic and could never accept the fact that people had flaws. Especially not me. He thought I was lazy and sloppy and that I needed to get my act together.

"So, did he also hit you when you were married?" Sophia asked, like she had read my thoughts.

"He would push me, or maybe slap me now and then. But it wasn't anything like this." I removed the icepack and showed Sophia the bruise Michael had left on my cheek.

"That's how it begins," Sophia said. "No guy ever starts out beating the crap out of you. He needs to know that you're not going to run anywhere first. Once he gets comfortable with you, that's when he shows his true colors. And if you don't leave him when the first slaps fall, then he'll continue, and it will get worse and worse. That's my experience anyway."

I looked at Maya, who was listening in on the conversation. Usually, I wouldn't want her to listen to stuff like this, but I had a feeling it would be good for her to hear. She was old enough to know. She had to have so many questions, the poor thing... so much confusion in her life. Was she ever going to come out of this as a whole person? Or was she damaged for life?

Sophia looked at her and smiled. "You hear me, honey. If he treats you bad... if he hits you, or even abuses you mentally or emotionally, you know... tells you you're no good, that you're wrong and need to change. That's when you leave him. You run and never look back. No matter how much you love him. You understand?"

Maya nodded while biting her lip.

"You don't just stay and take it because you think you have to or that he's right to do so. You run, all right?" Sophia continued.

"All right," Maya said, and sipped her hot chocolate.

"Otherwise, he'll peel you like an onion. He'll remove every layer of you till there's nothing left."

I felt terrible. That was exactly what Michael had done to me. He had started by criticizing me. Criticizing my every move. Everything I did or said. If we had guests, he would correct me afterward, telling me I was stupid for saying something that I had no idea what I was talking about. He would criticize everything I wore, tell me I looked chubby, and that I was lucky that he loved me because no one else would. And he hadn't done it all at once. No, it had come little by little over the years. It had been sneaking up on me, slowly diminishing my self-confidence, making me feel bad about myself, and making me think I was worthless.

How had I been so blind?

Now, he was doing the same to Victoria, and Maya had seen it. She had seen him beat her with his fist. That was why she had been angry. That was why she decided to run away.

I smiled at her and stroked her hair gently. My beautiful smart girl.

She knew she had to get away and not just take the abuse.

"What?" she asked.

"That has to have been the hardest decision in your life to make," I said. "To leave your dad. You had just moved there. You were angry with me for not telling you about your real dad. You wanted to move to be with the person who had been your father for all of your childhood, and then that happened. He turned out to be a bastard, treating your stepmother awfully, and then doing the same to you. So, you left. But where were you going? Do you remember?"

Maya shook her head. I could tell her brain was working overtime to try to figure it out. "I... I was going to see someone, when I hit..."

"You hit the man with your car. Do you remember it, or is it just because I've told you about it?"

Maya looked pensive. "I think... I think I do remember some of it. I remember the road, then flashes of light, and... something hitting the car. But that's all."

"At least it's something," I said. "But you still don't remember where you were going, do you?"

Maya shook her head. She had tears in her eyes. "I'm sorry."

"Don't be, honey," I said. "It'll come back to you. Maybe it isn't even important."

"No, I'm sorry for causing all this," she said.

"Are you kidding me? This is not your fault. You hear me? Nothing of this is your fault. Never ever think that it is!"

Maya didn't look like she was convinced. Her eyes hit the table and she seemed burdened by guilt. "What if I hadn't run out on dad like that? Maybe if I hadn't tried to stop him from hurting Victoria... what if I had never moved there? None of this would have happened."

"Still, not your fault," I said.

"Honey, there are bastards everywhere," Sophia said. "And they will always be bastards, no matter what you do and what you think you could've done different. You didn't make him a bastard. You didn't make him beat his wife... or you. That was his choice. It's his choice to be a freaking bastard."

Sophia's words seemed to do the job in Maya.

Maya smiled and nodded. "Thanks," she said.

"Any time, sweetheart," Sophia continued. "But, remember, not all men are pigs. Take Jack here. He's a find. You find yourself a man like him, and you've lucked out. They don't grow on trees, but they're out there if you look carefully."

Jack blushed while Sophia put her arm around him. I noticed something between them I hadn't seen before... a look in their eyes when they looked at each other.

My phone vibrated on the table, and I checked the display. It was Morten. He had called several times in the past half hour, but I hadn't picked up. I didn't feel like fighting, and I was angry with him for not calling or anything at all yesterday.

"Aren't you going to take that?" Sophia asked. "It's the third time today. Maybe it's important."

I exhaled. "Okay." I grabbed the phone and took it.

"Emma?" Morten sounded agitated.

"You won't believe what happened here," I said.

"You won't believe what happened here either."

I froze. Something bad had happened? I could tell it was urgent by the tone of his voice.

"What's going on?" I asked.

"There has been another one. Another double homicide. Spouses killed on the first night in their new home."

THIRTY-THREE

JUNE 2009

"You have lost your mind!"

Louise's mom looked at her and shook her head. "What have we done to make you do this to us? Have we been such bad parents?"

It was two days after the wedding. Unfortunately, Louise's parents hadn't kept their promise to stay away from her. As a matter of fact, they hadn't gotten off her back ever since the news spread that she was now Mrs. Lund. They kept calling her, and now they had come to her flat. Louise had let them in, but now she regretted it.

On the table in front of her lay the newspaper. Louise's picture was on the front cover.

WHO MARRIES A MURDERER?

Louise didn't care what they wrote about her. She didn't care what her parents thought, or if they were embarrassed by what she had done.

"I love him, Mom," she simply said, over and over again.

"Nonsense," her mother replied. "You are obviously going

through a phase of some sort. I talked to Doctor Wognsen. He thinks you're being rebellious against us. You're doing this to make us angry."

Louise scoffed. She didn't care what that stupid doctor thought. He was just an old fool. She wondered how a man like him could call himself a psychiatrist. She had seen him when she was in her late teens. All he did was prescribe new medicine for her. He never listened to what she told him. He would let her talk, but then tell her she needed her dose adjusted. It was his answer to everything.

At one point in time, Louise suspected that her mother paid him to just drug her and make her more manageable. Her mother always found it hard to control Louise.

Well, here you go, Mom. Try to control this. Ha!

"Why aren't you saying anything, Hans?" her mother asked, looking at Louise's dad.

Her father shook his head. "Maybe we should just..." He exhaled when he saw the look on his wife's face. Louise knew that look. He didn't want the bother.

"Just what?" she asked. "Maybe we should just what, Hans?"

"Nothing. It was nothing."

"I truly hope it was," she said, and adjusted her skirt. "I don't know what has gotten into you lately. Both of you. It's like I hardly know you anymore."

Louise's mom leaned over on the couch, where she and Louise were both sitting. Then she pinched Louise on the arm, like she had always done when she had no idea how to make Louise behave.

"Ouch!" Louise screamed.

Her mother then slapped her. "Behave, child. Behave."

Louise rose to her feet. "That really hurt, Mom."

Her mother snorted. "Well, it's your own fault for being so rebellious. I can't believe you married that guy. Now I have to clean up your mess for you, don't I? Just like I always have. You're such a mess, Louise. Can't you do anything right?"

Louise felt the anger rise in her again. Bjarke had told her she shouldn't let her mom talk to her like this. Not anymore. But it was hard... so hard for her to talk back to her mother. She had never dared to before.

"I have done something right. For once in my life, I have done something that makes me happy," Louise said, and stomped her feet on the carpet.

"Don't raise your voice at me," her mother snorted. "And stomping your feet like that on top of it. What is happening to you? It must be that condition of yours. I'll have to have Doctor Wognsen prescribe some new medicine for you. Yes, that's just what you need. Do sit back down, dear. You can't take being upset like this. It's too much for you."

She patted the seat next to her. "Sit here, sweetheart. Let Mommy take care of you. I know it's been a rough time for you. You need your mommy here. I'm not leaving anymore. I'll stay the night, if that's what it takes to make you feel better."

"I'm not sick, Mom. Look at the ring on my finger. That means I'm married. I'm a grown woman. I can take care of myself from now on. My husband will help me if I need anything."

Her mother burst into a loud and very high-pitched laughter. The sound cut through Louise's bones.

"Your husband, ha! Listen to her, Hans. Her husband. As if someone could ever love you. You have no idea what love is. And no one in his right mind would ever be able to love someone with your condition, someone unbalanced like you. You need to understand one thing, Louise. You're not like everybody else. There is something seriously wrong with your head. Am I right, Hans?"

She looked at Louise's dad, who nodded.

"Isn't that what the doctors have always told us?" she asked.

Hans nodded again.

"Well, there you go. Your dad agrees. You can never live a normal life, and frankly, marrying that guy proves to me that you are not at all right in your mind. To think you had to seduce a murderer, the scum of the earth, in order to get someone to marry you. Well, it's just plain pathetic, isn't it? Isn't it, Hans? Tell her. Tell her how pathetic she is."

THIRTY-FOUR

JULY 2014

There was another one? I sat down on a chair in my kitchen, completely paralyzed. The others were staring at me. I had put the phone down after Morten said goodbye.

"What's wrong, Mom?" Maya asked.

Sophia and Jack both watched me intensely.

"Yeah, you look awful, no offense," Sophia said.

"There was another one," I said.

"Another what?" Jack asked.

Sophia understood. She went quiet. "I think I'll get the whiskey," she finally said, and stood up.

"It's eleven o'clock," Jack said. "Don't you think it's a little early for that?"

Sophia found three glasses and put them on the table. Then she poured some whiskey for all of us. "So, where was it this time?" she asked. "Don't tell me it was another one on our street?"

I shook my head. "It was downtown. On the small street behind the church. I guess that's why it was blocked this morning when Michael was driving here."

Jack stared at me. I guessed he had finally figured out what we were talking about.

Maya was curious. "Was it like the neighbors?" she asked.

I nodded. "A couple. Killed in their new home on their first night there."

I'd decided it was okay for her to know about this. But I still wanted to protect her, because she'd been going through quite a lot lately.

"Maya, go check on your brother, will you?" I said. There was no reason for her to hear all this in detail. She had enough on her plate.

Maya sighed. "Really, Mom?"

"Yes, really. I want to make sure he's all right. Someone was killed on our island last night, and it scares me."

"I'm not a baby, you know. I can hear this stuff without getting scared," Maya protested.

It didn't help. I was about to share details about this killing that I didn't want her to hear.

"Please?" I said.

"Okay," Maya sighed demonstratively and left. I knew she wanted to be one of the adults, but there had to be a limit.

"So, what did Morten tell you?" Sophia asked.

I tasted the whiskey. It was strong. Just what I needed right now, even if it was a little early. It calmed me. "They were killed last night, the police assume. There's no sign of breaking and entering; the killer didn't force his way in."

"Who found them?"

"Believe it or not," I said. "It was Peter, the curtain guy again. This time, he didn't walk in. They had ordered new curtains. The wife had already chosen the fabric, but Peter had just gotten a new fabric shipment from Thailand and wanted to show it to her, in case she wanted to change her mind. The door to the house was slightly ajar, and when he realized that, he didn't dare to enter.

Not after what happened the other day. He called the police right away, and Morten was first officer on the scene. It was ugly, he said. Blood smeared on the walls and in the bed. Lots of blood. Both had been stabbed to death. The guy's throat was sliced."

"Was she wearing shoes?" Sophia asked.

I nodded. "Exact same type of shoes. Ruby red slippers."

"Like the film," Jack said.

I stared at him, while my thoughts wandered. I kept thinking about Victor's nightmare last night. It made sense. This killer had some sort of weird obsession with the classic film *The Wizard of Oz*. It wasn't a groundbreaking discovery, but it was something. It was a start.

THIRTY-FIVE

JULY 2014

Sunday, Morten came over for breakfast. I hadn't told him about the incident with my ex-husband but was planning to once he got here. He didn't notice the bruise on my cheek. I felt as if he hardly looked at me at all. He was exhausted from yesterday, he told me, and sat down with a deep sigh. I served freshly baked bread with cheese and butter.

"Do you have jam?" he asked.

He loved my homemade raspberry jam, and I still had one jar left in my cabinet. I pulled it out and gave it to him. "Last one," I said with a smile.

"Ah, I love this stuff," he said, and threw a big scoop on his bread and took a bite.

"I know you do."

"Is everything okay?" he asked. The jam was stuck in several of his teeth.

"I had a couple of tough days," I said. I didn't feel like talking about my encounter with Michael after all. Morten didn't seem genuinely interested in my answer anyway.

"Tell me about it," he said, and took another bite. "I'm

exhausted. Yesterday was rough." He stopped chewing and washed the food down with coffee.

"Why didn't you call me?" I asked, hearing how every word I said was loaded with disappointment and hurt.

He looked confused. "What? Call you when?"

"Friday. I didn't hear anything from you until Saturday morning."

Morten looked like he was trying to think back. "I'm not following you."

"I wanted you to call, or at least text me and say good night, on Friday after the party. You knew I was at home waiting. You knew I was upset about that party and not being invited."

Morten rolled his head back and massaged his neck. "I'm really not up for this," he said with a deep exhale. "Between you and Jytte, it's getting quite exhausting. There's always someone nagging me about something. I can never do right by either of you anymore. I'm getting sick of it, to be frank. On top of it, this case is killing me. This killer leaves no traces and no clues. Just a bloody scene of true devastation. It's unbearable. I have no energy to be fighting with you."

I looked at him. I could tell he was upset. But it wasn't because of me or Jytte, was it? It was something else. Something deeper.

"Are you okay?" I asked.

Morten looked at me. He was crying. "I... I..."

I put my arm around him. He pushed it away. "Morten. Talk to me. Is everything all right?"

"I... she... she was pregnant, Emma. He killed her in cold blood, undressed her and put on those awful shoes. She was carrying a little life inside of her. Who would do something like this?"

I leaned back in my chair. I was startled. Shocked. "I... I had no idea. How terrible. How truly awful."

Morten pushed his plate to the middle of the table and got up. "I don't think I can do this anymore," he said.

I stared at him. I couldn't believe what he was telling me. "What do you mean?" I asked, my voice shaking. "What are you saying?"

"I can't do this anymore. Any of it. It's too much for one guy to handle. I'm sorry, Emma. I need some time to think. I need a break from us, from all this... I..."

He looked around like he was searching for something. He paused. I didn't like the silence. It was like he was making an important decision. It scared me like crazy. I wanted to yell at him, to talk sense into him, tell him to sit down so we could talk properly like we used to. We always used to be able to talk things over. Why couldn't we do that now? What had happened to us?

I wanted to say all those things, but I waited too long. Before I knew it, he looked at me and said the words I didn't want to hear.

"I need to go."

THIRTY-SIX
JULY 2014

Jesper Melander was on fire. Everything was just going perfectly, wasn't it? Just perfectly. Even better than he had ever imagined. The gruesomeness of his killings was all over the newspapers this Monday morning, and he could hardly contain his joy. He couldn't keep it inside. He burst into a giggle and started clapping.

He felt like a genius... a freaking composer directing his orchestra.

The newspapers called him a beast, a predator, a monster, and a psychopath. On TV, they had experts telling people about his motives, analyzing him.

Boy, they couldn't be more wrong.

He loved the fact that he was the one orchestrating this whole thing; they had no idea how he was pulling the strings, making sure they only saw what he wanted them to see.

And he had never felt more alive.

He threw the newspaper with Jacob and Christine Hansen's faces on the cover on the passenger seat, then looked out the window across the street. A smile spread across his face.

There they were. He spotted them in the distance, walking toward the house.

"There you are, my little ones," he mumbled. "That's right. Look at the house, fall in love. Pay no attention to the man behind the curtain."

The couple looked at the front door, then the windows, then walked back and forth a little. Jesper could see that the wife liked it. The husband wasn't so sure, but he wanted to please the wife. He wanted her to be happy.

"Look at those beautiful small-paned windows. They're gorgeous," Jesper Melander said, trying to sound like the woman.

Speaking in a deep voice, trying to sound like the husband, he said, "Yes. They are nice, but not very practical. Think of how hard they'll be to clean."

"Oh, but honey. It's such a pretty house. I really like it, don't you? Would you buy me this house? I think we could be very happy here." He continued in a high-pitched female voice.

Then, he laughed at himself. It was amazing how all the couples were so alike. So boringly similar. Lucky for them, he was about to make them more than that. Yes, Jesper was about to make them spectacular.

The hairs on his arm rose at the very thought. Oh, what a joy this was. He wished he could go on with this forever and ever. It was the most fun he'd had in his entire life. Who would have thought it would be such an exciting experience? Such a thrill? He knew it was close to his latest kill, and he wanted to make sure they were absolutely perfect before he acted on it. He didn't want to rush this and risk making a mistake, but when opportunity knocks... well, then he should grab it, right?

Jesper grabbed the steering wheel in excitement and held on to it tight. His knuckles were turning white while he was humming one of his favorite songs from his favorite film of all time.

* * *

Jesper tasted blood in his mouth and realized his nose had started bleeding. He let go of the steering wheel, found a napkin, and wiped off the blood. He liked the pattern it made on the napkin. It looked like flowers as it was spreading slowly.

He looked at himself in the rearview mirror, then chuckled. He crumpled the napkin up and threw it on the floor of the car, then his eyes returned to the waiting couple outside the small yellow house that they seemed to adore.

Jesper Melander studied them closely. They really seemed to like the house already, didn't they? He could tell by the looks on their faces. And they hadn't even seen it on the inside yet. The wife was smiling. But, more important, so was the husband. He was the one sitting on the money. In the end, he was going to make the final decision. It could take days, maybe even weeks, but Jesper would wait for them. He wasn't in a hurry. It had to be them. It was like waiting for an apple to become ripe. The thought and anticipation of how juicy it would be to sink his teeth into it was almost the best part.

Well, almost.

Jesper's legs couldn't stay still in the car. He was tapping them in excitement. Oh, this couple was so perfect. Especially her. She was beautiful, gorgeous actually, and would make a wonderful corpse. She wasn't beautiful in the way most people found a woman to be beautiful. But to Jesper, she was striking. He liked them fierce and raw. He could already picture her photo on the cover of his newspaper. Best of all were her small delicate feet. He couldn't think of a better set of feet to wear the shoes, his shoes. Oh, what a delight. How he hoped they would buy this house.

It would be so much FUN!

THIRTY-SEVEN

AUGUST 2014

Three weeks later, my kids were going back to school. I was thrilled at the prospect of being able to finally get some work done while they were away, but I was terrified to send Maya back there without her memory.

A couple of days before school started, I had a meeting with her teachers and the principal at the school and made them aware of her situation. They promised me that Maya would get extra care, and they would do anything in their power to help her. They were surprisingly kind and encouraging, and it made me slightly more at ease.

Still, I had no idea how she was supposed to manage in class when she remembered absolutely nothing of school.

"Maybe it'll come back to her once she gets back into her familiar surroundings," Dr. Faaborg told me, when I called in desperation and asked him how I was supposed to deal with this.

"But she doesn't remember anything. She can read and write, that's it. She has no recollection of things they've learned, of books she has read, and doing maths with her is like starting all over from scratch."

"She might remember things along the way. The important thing is not to panic. She'll be fine eventually," he said.

"I sure hope so."

"Don't worry so much. It's not helping Maya. Take one day at a time. By the way, how is the book coming along? I'll get my signed copy, right?"

I chuckled. Dr. Faaborg was one of my biggest fans. "Don't worry so much, doctor."

Now I was standing in the doorway, kissing both of the kids goodbye, and wondering how it had all come to this point. I hadn't seen or heard from Morten since the day he left me in my kitchen alone with a half-eaten jam sandwich and the words "I don't think I can do this anymore."

I knew he was working on the case of the two double homicides. I had followed the investigation closely by hacking into the Danish police force computer system that, to my surprise, remained very poorly protected. I had seen forensic reports from the second kill, and it was all still a mystery to everyone who was behind this. Luckily, there hadn't been any more killings for three weeks, and I hoped it was over, that the killer maybe had been just passing through or maybe he was done. Maybe it had been a revenge motive of some sort, and now he was done. I just couldn't see the connection between the two sets of victims. The couples didn't know each other, and all they had in common was the fact that they were newlyweds and had just bought their first houses. In the first case, the killer had taken the husband's heart; in the second, he had cut out the husband's brain. The nature of the killings was so gruesome it made the hairs stand up on my back just by thinking about them. I had searched everywhere to see if there were cases similar to these two but hadn't found anything yet.

"Don't worry, Mom. I'll be fine," Maya said and kissed me. Then she walked down the stairs with her backpack. I had some serious butterflies in my stomach. I could tell by the look in her eyes that she was nervous as well. She just didn't want me to know. She didn't want me to worry.

"I know, sweetie," I replied, and waved at her as she took her bike and rode off. I had taken the trip to the school with her on our bikes every day for a week to make sure she knew the route and wasn't concerned about biking to school. At first, I told her I would drive her, but she found that to be extremely embarrassing, because all the other kids rode their bikes to school.

Even Victor.

At nine years old, he was getting so tall I could hardly believe he was the same little boy. He drove off with a wave.

"Have a great day!" I yelled after him.

"You always say that," he yelled back.

So, that was it. I was alone. The silence was nice, but a little unbearable. Luckily, Sophia had the day off and didn't start working until the next day. She worked part-time as a music teacher at Victor's school and only had to work three days a week. All of her six kids were back in school and daycare, and she wanted to celebrate by us going out for a nice brunch together.

I couldn't think of a better way to spend the day.

THIRTY-EIGHT

AUGUST 2014

"Could it have something to do with that curtain guy?"

Sophia took a bite of her salmon sandwich while I spoke.

"I mean, it is kind of weird that he was the one to find both of them, right?"

Sophia swallowed and shook her head. "What is it with you and those killings? It's like you're obsessed with them. Leave it alone already. It's been three weeks. It's over. He's gone."

I drank my Coke. Café Mimosa had some new paintings on the walls. They were all Jack's. They had ocean and beach motifs. I loved all of them. He used such wonderful colors and captured the light just perfectly in them. On the table behind us sat Lisa Rasmussen, a member of the city council who was having a meeting with two other members. She was talking very loudly. It sounded like she was talking to a crowd of children, but it was to two adults. She sounded really annoyed with them. The election for mayor was coming up this fall, and she was running. I had never cared much for her, but she had done a very good job cleaning up the town and our beaches. I had to give her that much. I almost laughed, thinking about the time Lisa Rasmussen had taken down a killer in this very same café.

It was quite impressive. Maybe I would give her my vote after all. I didn't know. I was indecisive about her. She seemed a little mad to me, but maybe that wasn't such a bad thing in politics. She got the work done, that was for sure.

"Maybe you're right," I said. "Maybe I should just let it go. I just can't stop thinking about it."

"You just want to write a book about it," Sophia said, laughing.

"I really do," I said. "Is that terrible? I often feel like I'm exploiting these people's tragedy."

"Nah," Sophia said. "You're a great writer. It's what you do. You should be proud of it. At least something good comes out of them dying."

I chuckled. Sophia could always get something positive out of everything. I had known her almost two years now, and I had really grown to love her. I knew she would always be there for me. That was worth a whole lot in my book.

"But it is kind of a strange coincidence that they both used the same curtain guy, don't you think?" I asked.

Sophia grinned. "You just can't leave it alone, can you? All right, let's get it out. So, you think this curtain guy, what's his name?

"Peter Wagn."

"Peter Wagn. You seriously think he did it, then returned to the scene and fainted?"

I shrugged. "Why not? It is, after all, the perfect alibi. No one would ever suspect him. This killer is cunning, if you ask me. Peter could be playing a role... pretending to be fragile. Plus, serial killers have been known to return to the scene of the crime afterward. They like to look at their work. At least that's what Morten has told me. And we're looking for a guy who knows that these people just bought a house, right? Well, the curtain guy knew."

Sophia nodded while chewing. "True. But so did the

moving company, the contractors, the real estate agent, just to mention a few. Besides, the Curtain Company is the only one of its kind on the island, so it's not that strange that they both would call it. Just bad luck for poor Peter Wagn."

She made a good point. Lots of people were involved when buying a new home.

"I can't stop thinking about the shoes," I said. "I mean, where do you even buy a pair of shoes like that? Let alone two pairs?"

"I've been thinking the same thing," Sophia exclaimed. "These aren't ordinary shoes."

"Thank you! Morten laughed at me every time I brought it up. Told me I was such a girl."

"Any news on that front?" Sophia asked.

I paused and drank. Then I shook my head. "Not a word. I can't believe he would just walk out on me this way."

"You miss him?"

"Yeah. Like crazy. But I've been a good girl. Only called him three times and hung up."

"That's my girl. Give him time."

I sighed. That was exactly what I was trying to do. But it was so hard. Especially when I knew he was so close by. Every day, I had to fight the urge to just drop by, either at his home or at the police station. I kept coming up with excuses for going there, but so far, I had been able to keep my cool and stay away. Besides, I had no idea what to say to him. I just hoped he missed me as much as I missed him. But as the days passed by without a word from him, I doubted it more and more.

"Any news from the ex?" Sophia asked.

"A letter from his lawyer, if that counts as news," I said. "He's demanding full custody of Victor. Can you believe him? Two years ago, the guy told me he couldn't handle him, and that it was too much for his new wife to have him for even a weekend. Now he wants him full-time?"

"So, did you respond to the letter?"

"I did. I told them I'd take it all the way to court if I had to. He wasn't getting anywhere near my child."

"That's my girl."

THIRTY-NINE
AUGUST 2014

It was first day of school for all the kids in the country. Facebook was packed with pictures of happy children wearing their backpacks and nice outfits and their even happier parents.

The numerologist loved this day, even though she didn't have any children. It was the fourth of August, so the day's number was three. Three was a good number. Perfect for a new beginning, and that was exactly what the numerologist was about to have.

Today, she started the second part of her plan. She had studied Emma Frost and found her weaknesses. Now it was time to use that knowledge.

It was just about to get interesting.

She had watched the house since the morning when the kids left for school, and later when Emma took her bike to town along with that annoying neighbor of hers who had six kids.

Six kids? Didn't the woman have any self-control?

Now, she watched as Emma and Sophia returned and said their goodbyes. The numerologist looked at her watch. There were only fifteen minutes till the kids came home. The first day was a short day. Emma had a bag in her hand. She had been shopping. It looked like she had bought herself a pair of shoes.

Misty was nibbling on a piece of bread in the passenger seat next to her.

"I know you're sad, Misty, darling. But you can't go. No, you can't. They won't allow rats in there with me. They probably wouldn't even let me come inside if they saw you. Yes, Mommy knows you always come with me everywhere, but this time you just can't, all right? You have to stay in the car till I get back. This has to be perfect to succeed."

The numerologist looked at her new face in the mirror once again. She still hadn't gotten used to looking so differently.

I just hope they won't recognize me. What if they can see it in my eyes? What if I lose one of the colored contacts?

"Nonsense," she told herself in the mirror. "They won't suspect a thing. The plan is perfect."

The numerologist picked up the rat and pet her on the back. Then she kissed it on the snout. The whiskers tickled her face. The numerologist thought about Emma Frost and her children. She realized she had grown to like them more than she wanted to. She felt a pinch of sadness in her heart. It was always the children who got hurt in the process, wasn't it?

"Well, I guess that's not our problem, is it, Misty? It wasn't like Emma Frost thought about what it cost us when she destroyed our baby, was it? No, she ruined years of research without even thinking about how much it meant to us. Yes, indeed, she did."

Misty answered with a squeak. The numerologist tickled her stomach. She had recently read in a study from Washington State University that rats could actually laugh when tickled on their stomachs, so she had been doing that to Misty a lot lately. Misty seemed to love it but hadn't made a sound yet. The numerologist really wanted to hear her rat laugh.

"Laugh for Mommy. Come on, Misty, you can do it. Oh, come on. Just a little giggle for Mommy?"

But the rat didn't laugh this time either. The numerologist gave up.

She looked at the clock. It was almost one.

One. The perfect number. The number of creation, the primal force from which all other numbers spring forth. One was aggressive; a powerful force that produced results and didn't allow anything or anyone to limit its potential. One was a number that walked upright with pride and purpose. It was strong, determined, unwavering. A one could turn dreams and ideas into reality.

It was also the time that both of Emma's children were done with school. The numerologist waited only a few minutes before both of them rode their bikes into the driveway of the house. She watched them walk inside.

She waited about fifteen minutes more before she got out of the car, and, with the pride of the number one, she walked upright and with purpose toward the front door.

FORTY

AUGUST 2014

I was late. Sophia and I had finished our brunch and then gone shoe shopping. I had talked to a woman in a shoe shop and asked her if they had any red shoes. She had found a high-heeled pair that I tried on. I liked them and ended up buying them. As I paid, I asked the woman casually if she knew how to get a hold of a pair of shoes like the ones Dorothy wore in *The Wizard of Oz*.

"I don't have any here in the shop, but you can buy them online, I'm sure. I would do that if it was me."

"Of course," I said, and paid for my own pair of red shoes. It made sense to buy them online. That way, he could get them without anyone noticing it. It would be something a salesperson would remember if a guy came in and bought two pairs of ruby red slippers. Our killer was way too clever to be seen like that.

I put away my new shoes in the wardrobe upstairs and hurried down to the kitchen. I had prepared dough to make a cake for the kids when they got home... to celebrate the first day of school. All I had to do was bake it in the oven for twenty minutes, and then I had to make the topping from coconut flakes and brown sugar. It was an old classic that went by the name of Danish Dream Cake. It was the kids' favorite.

I made hot chocolate to go with it for the kids and coffee for myself. I had barely taken the cake out of the oven and started making the topping when Victor stormed through the front door.

"Hi, buddy. How was the first day of school?"

Victor didn't look at me. I was used to that, but this was different. He seemed upset. "Did something happen?" I asked, and squatted in front of him, trying to look him in the eyes.

He was breathing heavily. "Someone took my favorite rock," he said.

"Who did?" I asked.

"Mrs. Rasmussen."

"Your maths teacher. Why did she take your rock?" I asked.

"Because I kept telling all the answers. She said the other kids won't learn anything if I keep yelling the answers."

"Victor. You know you have to raise your hand like all the other children. We've been through this so many times."

"Yes. But she never picks me. And the other children are too slow. It's so easy, and they never get it right. When they get it wrong, I tell them the answer. What's wrong with that?"

I sighed. "So, the teacher punished you by taking your favorite rock, huh?"

"Then I got really mad, and she sent me to the principal's office. They'll probably call you later today, the principal told me."

"On the first day, huh? Well, that was fast. Any good news?"

"They have my favorite ice cream at the cafeteria now."

"Which one is your favorite?" I asked.

But Victor had lost interest in the conversation and walked right past me and sat down at the table. He took out his notebook and started writing in it. I was amazed at how fast he was able to write. He was always writing in it, but seldom let me see it. I tried to look over his shoulder while serving him his hot chocolate, but he was covering it up with his hand and thick curly hair.

Seconds later, Maya stepped in. My heart rate went up. I had been so nervous for her. She walked inside the kitchen and threw herself into a chair. She hardly looked at me.

Uh-oh!

"How was your day, sweetheart?" I asked cautiously.

She looked up at me. I could tell she had been crying. It broke my heart. Maya covered her face with her hands.

"Maya, honey? What happened?"

"I'm never going back. I don't remember anything! I don't remember anyone. Everybody was staring at me and pointing fingers and I had no idea who they were or if I knew them or not. I didn't even know who used to be my friends. It was awful. I'm never going back. I'll stay home forever."

I put my hand on her shoulder. "I'm sorry," I said. "I'm so, so sorry. What about Annika? She used to be your best friend; didn't she help you?"

"Yes. She was very nice to me. But I feel weird around her. I feel like I don't know her. And we're so different. I don't think we have anything in common. I'm not even sure I like her. I can't believe she used to be my best friend. What is happening to me, Mom? Have I changed that much?"

I put my arm around her and pulled her closer. "I don't know, sweetie. I think you're just trying to find yourself right now... figure out who you really are."

I held her for a little while longer, wondering if she really had changed. I felt it too. She was different somehow. Was it just a phase? Would she pull through it, or was it here to stay?

Maya sniveled and I wiped away a tear. "It was terrible, Mom. I didn't remember anything. It was hard to understand what the teacher was saying. Maths was the worst."

"Well, maths was never your strongest subject," I said.

The clock on the oven beeped. "I made dream cake," I said, trying hard to sound cheerful.

Victor didn't react. Maya sniveled again. "I think I need to study. I'm not hungry anyway."

She got up and left the kitchen. Victor stopped writing, closed the notebook, and put it in his backpack, then stormed out of the kitchen without so much as a word. I looked at the cake on the counter. It smelled so good. I shrugged and cut myself a piece, then grabbed a cup of coffee and started eating. My stomach was in a knot. I felt like crying, but I didn't. Eating the cake made me feel better, so I grabbed another piece. I thought about Morten, about Michael my ex-husband, about the killings, and my poor children. I felt awful, so I grabbed another piece and more coffee. It wasn't like I had anyone in my life I needed to lose those pounds for anyway. It didn't matter anymore.

Was that why he left me? Did he finally have enough of my eating and gaining weight?

The thought made me eat more. With every bite I took, I felt more disgusted with myself, but I continued anyway. I could hear Morten's voice in my head telling me to stop, telling me I was overeating because I was emotional, that I was simply drowning my emotions with food. I knew he was right; I just didn't know what to do about it. I wasn't the type who cried when things were bad in my life. I just wasn't. This was what I did. Some people drank. I ate.

I would have eaten the entire cake, but had only managed about a third, when the doorbell suddenly rang. I swallowed the big bite I had just taken, drank some coffee to wash it down, and walked over to open the door. Part of me wished it was Morten who had come to say he wanted to come back, but I knew it wasn't him. I had hoped for weeks now that he would come, but in vain. I wasn't going to hope for it anymore. I had to focus on moving on, and right now I had bigger issues than him. I had to figure out what to do to help my daughter get back to being herself again. Maybe I could get her a tutor. Someone to help her get better at her schoolwork at least.

I pulled the door open and looked into the face of a pretty, widely smiling face of an Asian woman. There was something familiar about her, but I couldn't figure out what it was.

"Mrs. Frost?" she said.

"Yes?"

We shook hands.

"I'm very honored to meet you, Mrs. Frost. I have enjoyed and devoured every book you've written."

"Oh, well, thank you. What is your name?" I asked, thinking she was just a fan stopping by to tell me she loved my books. I'd had a few of those, especially over the summer when all the tourists came to the island. My books had recently been translated into German, and Fanoe island attracted a lot of German tourists, because it was close to the border.

"Sonnichsen. Doctor Sonnichsen."

"Well, Doctor Sonnichsen. Let me just get a pen."

The woman looked puzzled. "Excuse me?"

"To sign your book? I assume you brought one?" I asked.

The woman laughed. It sounded a little strange. I blushed slightly, realizing I had made a mistake.

"Oh, no, Mrs. Frost. I'm not here for you... even though I do like your books. I'm here for your daughter."

"For Maya? I don't think I understand..."

"I was sent here by your social worker. I'm an occupational therapist. My specialty field is children with amnesia."

I froze completely. Could this really be? Was there really an expert in amnesia patients right here on my front step? I was startled, baffled, blown away. I had searched for someone like her for months, but they were almost impossible to get ahold of.

"You say a social worker sent you?"

"Yes. Apparently, you contacted her regarding your daughter, um, Maya, is it?"

I nodded eagerly. "Yes. Yes I did. I called several times over the summer and left messages for her, but I had no idea she would actually react."

Dr. Sonnichsen chuckled. "Well, she did. I know people usually don't think much of our social welfare system, but, from time to time, it actually works pretty well. Your social worker talked to your doctor, Doctor Faaborg, and they agreed the best way to deal with this was to send me. So, here I am. And I'm all paid for by the region, so you don't have to worry about that. But enough talking. I've come here for Maya. I would like to meet her."

"Of course," I said. I was still staring, completely baffled, at the woman. I felt like I was dreaming.

"So, are you going to let me come in?"

"Naturally," I said, laughing at myself. I stepped aside immediately and let her walk inside my house. I stared at her while closing the door. I wanted to kiss her and hug her and tell her she was the answer to my prayers. I couldn't believe it. Finally, some luck was coming my way.

"She's upstairs studying. I'll go get her," I said, my voice vibrating with excitement. "You can wait in the kitchen if you like. I baked a cake. Help yourself to a piece."

FORTY-ONE
JANUARY 2010

"I'm coming home."

Louise was clasping the phone so hard her fingers started hurting. "What was that again?" she asked, her voice shivering.

"I'm being released," Bjarke said.

"But... but... how? Why?"

"They found the person who did it. They found the real killer. Isn't it wonderful? Finally, we can be together. Finally, it's just you and me."

Louise had no idea how to answer. After six months of being married to Bjarke, she had gotten used to the way things were. She liked visiting him every week, and even better, she liked that she always knew where he was. Now, that was about to change.

"Aren't you thrilled, babe?" he asked, his voice almost cracking in joy.

"S-s-s sure I am."

"Then, why don't you sound happy?"

"Guess I'm just really surprised, that's all."

"Me too. I can't believe it. They just told me a minute ago. Walked right into my cell and told me I was free to leave. I'm so

happy. You have no idea what it's like to sit in here for something you didn't do. I had given up hope. This is amazing. We
can finally start our life together."

"So, you... you are free to go, like, right now?" Louise asked.
Her hands were trembling.

*Everything is so good the way it is. Why does it have to
change?*

"Well, they have to finish the paperwork. I've been told that
I'll be released at noon."

"Noon? And then what?"

"Then I'll take the first train out of here. That way I can be
on Fanoe island by dinnertime. Would you make me a dinner,
Louise?"

Louise had no idea what to say. She wanted to throw the
phone away and start running. She had never been with Bjarke
for more than a few hours at a time. Now what? Now he was
coming here? Was he going to sleep here? Would he live here?
Did she dare to have him here?

*Stop it, you fool. You love him, remember? You believed he
was innocent from the start. Now he is. Be happy. He's your
husband.*

Louise closed her eyes and bit her lip. "Of course I will," she
said. "Do you like lasagna?"

"Are you kidding? I love lasagna. It's my favorite dish. Oh,
my, I can't believe this is really happening. Yeehaw. I'm free,
Louise. I'm free!"

"I... I can't believe it either. So who was it? Who killed your
ex-girlfriend and her kids?"

"Some nutjob. They haven't told me much about it. Actually, they didn't even tell me anything. Just that they were
letting me go. New development in the case, they said. I heard
something from another inmate. He told me he heard that they
had found new evidence incriminating someone else for it. I
guess it must have been pretty hard evidence, huh? What do I

care? I'm a free man. I can't wait to hold you in my arms, Louise. I can't wait to see your island that you've talked about so endearingly. I can't wait to get away from all this. You have no idea how depressing it is in here, Louise. But it's all in the past now. It's over. No more visiting hours. Now, we can be with each other all hours of the day. Just you and me, baby. Just you and me. Me and the missus."

"I... I... I can't wait."

Bjarke sighed deeply. "Oh, and by the way... I've changed my name. I don't want the world to look at me and see a murderer. 'Cause I know they will. Even if I'm released, they'll always see me that way, Louise. So, now, I'm a new person."

"Okay, so what's your name now?" she asked.

"Melander. Jesper Melander."

"Guess that makes me Mrs. Melander, huh?"

"I guess so."

"I like it."

FORTY-TWO
AUGUST 2014

Jesper Melander put the black slippers on a newspaper in the bathroom. It was important to use a well-ventilated place, or the smell would be awful.

Jesper shook the spray tin and sprayed the shoes, coloring them red, making sure it was even all over. He didn't want them to look cheap, or even homemade. Then, he set them to dry.

While waiting, Jesper looked at the listing on his computer... that lovely yellow house that now had the sign across its picture online that said that sweet, enchanting word: SOLD.

It had taken some time for the young couple to get the loan through the bank, and it almost fell through at one point. It had been quite the drama. But now, the house was finally theirs, and they were receiving the keys by the end of this week. The house had been vacant for two years, so they could take over right away.

Jesper could hardly wait.

It had been three weeks since his last kill, and he was getting hungry. It had been hard to restrain himself. It was like Pandora's box. He couldn't close it again. He couldn't hold back anymore. He needed to kill again, and even having to wait till the end of the week required all of his restraint, all of his self-control and discipline.

Ten hours later, he picked up the shoes and checked if the paint was dry. It was. He picked up the glue gun that was all warmed up and sat at the kitchen table. He grabbed the bag of large red sequins and dropped them on the table. Carefully, he placed a dab of hot glue on the tip of the shoe.

Don't use too much, or it'll look ugly. Don't want to have to start all over like the last time, do we?

With a pair of tweezers, he picked up a sequin and placed it in the glue.

Place them as close together as possible, but don't shove them together, you idiot!

Once the first was on, the rest were easier. Jesper placed another dab of hot glue, then placed a sequin on that as well. Then he smiled, while continuing. Soon, he was singing a song the lion in *The Wizard of Oz* sung about being afraid.

The shoes were coming along fine now. Slowly, those boring ordinary black shoes became sparkling and red, looking like those from a fairy tale.

"Oh, you're going to look so pretty, my angel, wearing the ruby red slippers from your dreams. Never prettier... never prettier, they'll write in the newspapers. Yes, they will. They'll write that she was so beautiful... quiet and peaceful, naked, dressed in nothing but the most enchanting ruby red slippers, lying on top of the bed in her new home. There certainly is no place to die like in your home. East or west, home is best. Isn't it, dearie? It sure is. It sure is."

Jesper lifted the sparkling shoes into the air, and then shook them to see if any sequins were loose. He held them up to the light and smiled.

FORTY-THREE
AUGUST 2014

Dr. Sonnichsen came every afternoon all week. She spent hours with Maya in the living room, going through what she remembered and what she didn't, taking notes and assessing her.

I was just thrilled. Maya seemed to be doing much better already. She hadn't come home crying again, and she looked forward to spending time with Dr. Sonnichsen. I had no idea how long we would have her, but I was hoping it would be a long time.

On Friday, she arrived, as usual, right before Maya came home from school, and we all had afternoon tea together. Then, they moved to the living room and began their work.

I had decided not to meddle but was incredibly curious as to what they were doing. Later that day, Dr. Sonnichsen finally decided to enlighten me a little.

She came into the kitchen where I was preparing dinner and sat down.

"So, to keep you updated, I can tell you that I have now observed Maya for a couple of days and tried to figure out exactly how much she remembers and where she has gaps. I have to say, there are a lot of gaps... putting it mildly. But, that doesn't mean she can't fill those out in time. But it will take just that... time."

I wiped my fingers on my apron and sat down. My stomach turned into a knot, wondering how much time it would take.

"I know you want to know how long it's going to take," Dr. Sonnichsen continued, as if she had read my mind. "But, as a habit, I never try to estimate a timeframe for the simple reason that each child is very different, and every case is different. It might take weeks; it might take even years. I don't know."

Years?!

Everything inside of me was screaming desperately. Was this thing going to go on for years?

"And, you must know that there is such a thing as permanent amnesia. Not all patients regain their memory completely. That is, of course, only in the very severe cases," she continued.

"Is Maya severe?" I asked, my voice shaking.

Dr. Sonnichsen exhaled. "Who can say? All I can tell you is that I intend to work with her from now on, and we'll just have to see."

"Okay. Okay," I said, even though I wanted to scream in frustration. I needed better answers, clearer answers. I needed to know that my daughter would be herself... and preferably very soon.

"So, you'll work with her, here in this house every day... or?" I asked.

"Yes. I'll start a more intensive program this Monday. I have great hopes for Maya."

I closed my eyes in relief. At least she had good hopes. That was something. It was a start.

"For how long? How long will you be able to work with her?" I asked anxiously.

Dr. Sonnichsen smiled. There was something about that smile that reminded me of someone. I couldn't figure out who it was.

"As long as it takes," she said.

"As long as it takes?" I asked, baffled. "As in, no limits? What if it takes years for her to get better?"

"That is very rare," she said. "The children I work with usually regain around eighty percent of their memory within three to four months, but that varies a lot, naturally. It cannot be forced. We must give it the time it takes for the brain to heal. It's a very delicate matter, the memory, and we must take it one day at a time. Let's see where it takes us, shall we?"

Dr. Sonnichsen looked at me intensely. I felt comfortable in her presence. I was happy to put my daughter in her hands.

She rose to her feet and put on her jacket. "I'll start with the memory training for Maya on Monday. At first, we'll focus on helping her with day-to-day tasks, help her organize herself to avoid further confusion in her life right now. She needs all the stability she can get. I'll let you know that the children I usually work with have what we call dissociative amnesia, a condition triggered by trauma. I've never worked with someone with drugged-induced amnesia before. I do, however, think that Maya's reactions will be very similar to those of my other patients."

"And, what are those reactions, usually?" I asked.

"She might get introverted from time to time, even draw away from you and your family; she could get angry, aggressive, or refuse to speak at all. Those are very common reactions. She's not in a good place right now, and she can't explain to others what is happening, as she doesn't understand it herself. Be aware of signs of a beginning depression as well. But, do promise me you won't treat her as if she's sick. She is not ill. It is vital that you try to keep a normal life for her. Keep her in school. Have her be with her friends. Talk to her friends and tell them she doesn't understand everything, and that she has a hard time remembering things. It might bother them, or even hurt them, that she can't remember them, but explain to them it's not personal. She's just going through a rough time. Provide a secure and caring environment at home. Make her feel useful. Give her some chores that she can handle easily."

Dr. Sonnichsen gave me a friendly smile.

"I... I can't thank you enough," I said. "You have no idea how much I've prayed for help. You're heaven sent."

"Well, I don't know about that. But I'm glad that I can be of help to you in this difficult time. See you on Monday."

"See you then."

FORTY-FOUR
AUGUST 2014

They had bought a house. Finally, Camilla and Mikkel had been able to agree on something. Ever since they met each other in a club in Esbjerg, they had fought about everything. It could even be the littlest things, like what to eat or how to spend the weekend.

So, naturally, finding a house, the right house, had taken them almost a year. They were both fed up with looking and searching for the right one, so when the yellow house on the south side of Fanoe island showed up, and they actually, finally, agreed, they threw in an offer as fast as possible. The bank almost said no, because Camilla wanted to start up her own business as a tattoo artist. The lenders didn't believe in that idea very much, plus, she had a lot of debt from traveling around Asia, charging everything on her credit cards, and never being able to pay it back.

But Mikkel had a decent job, and made an okay, stable, living. Enough for him to be able to vouch for her. He told the bank that he was good for the money, and they knew he was, because his parents owned a big house on the mainland. They knew he would eventually inherit enough money to pay their debts, if necessary.

So, finally, they were able to move into their new house and begin a brand-new life for themselves. It was in Sønderho, the second largest city on the island. A perfect place for the two of them to start all over.

They couldn't agree on whether to pay for a moving company or just do everything themselves. Camilla thought it would be nice to have people do the hard work for her, while Mikkel said they had to be sensible with their money now... that they couldn't just throw it around like she used to.

"We have a big car. We don't have much stuff anyway. We can fit it in my sister's minivan," he said. "We might have to make a few trips, but we'll still save a lot of money."

They fought about that for a couple of hours, and then settled on renting a moving lorry, so they only had to make the trip once.

Now they had moved all their stuff and were standing in their messy living room filled with boxes and bags. Mikkel grabbed two beers and handed one to Camilla.

"Light beer?" Camilla complained. "I hate light beer."

"Yeah, well, I love it," Mikkel said and opened his.

Camilla opened hers, as well, even if it was a little reluctantly. "To our new home," Mikkel said, as they toasted.

Then they drank. Camilla wiped away her black hair that was constantly in her face. Her tongue was playing with the new piercing in her lip. "I don't want the couch to be over here; I want it over there," she said, and pointed at the corner.

"What?" Mikkel said.

Camilla drank her beer. "That's the way it's gonna be, and you know it," she said, after swallowing.

"Never," Mikkel said.

"Why are you fighting me on this?" she asked. "You know I'll get my way at some point."

"No. Not about this. You got to choose that hideous couch. Now I want to say where it goes. If that thing is going to be in my living room, it has to be right there where I put it."

"Nope," she said.

"It will," he said.

"No, it won't," she said.

"I don't want it over there. That's the worst place to put a couch. You can hardly get past it and walk into the kitchen. Why don't you think before you speak?"

"Why don't you think?" Camilla said, mocking him.

But Mikkel didn't reply. Instead, he walked to the window and looked into the dusk.

"What are you doing?" Camilla asked. What was he up to? He was ruining a perfectly good fight.

"I think I saw something," he said.

Camilla scoffed. "Like what? There's nothing on this island."

"It looked like someone was looking in," he said.

"Let me see," Camilla said, and walked to the window in her black army boots. "Ah, there's nothing there."

"There was someone. I'm certain. I'm not lying to you," Mikkel said, his face turning red in distress. She always thought he was such a wuss. He hated that. "I'm not making this up."

"You're being ridiculous. No one is there," Camilla said. "Let's unpack a few more boxes and then go to bed."

FORTY-FIVE

AUGUST 2014

Mikkel grabbed a few more books from a box and put them on the shelf. Camilla was upstairs in the bedroom, making the bed so they could soon get some sleep. Mikkel was exhausted. He hated moving and hoped this was going to be the last time for many years. This was the place he wanted to stay; he wanted to have children here and grow old here. He wanted to grow old with Camilla.

Camilla was of a completely different opinion, of course. She wasn't ready to settle yet, she kept telling him. She wasn't like him. She wasn't able to stay in the same place for long. She would always tease him about being too sensible, so boring, and she would call him an old man in a young man's body. She wanted to live in many places, many different cities, and even different countries. Just the thought exhausted Mikkel even further.

But, he loved her. He loved her more than anyone he had ever had close to him in his life. He had no idea he was even capable of loving anyone this much. It was overwhelming. So, they fought a lot. It didn't matter. They kind of liked it. Both of them did. Camilla was feisty, and it was very good for Mikkel to be with her. She was the perfect counterpart.

She would keep him on his toes, and with her, he would never grow old and dull like his parents had.

That was his worst fear... ending up like them. He liked stability, yes, but there was a part of him that was almost as terrified of it as Camilla was. He had seen what it had done to his parents.

Mikkel smiled at the thought of their crazy wedding. It hadn't been exactly the way his mother had pictured it, that was for sure. It had been held at a graveyard, the music was death metal, and everyone had worn black. Even Camilla.

It had amused Mikkel to see his mother's face during the ceremony... her mouth looking like she had eaten a bitter lemon. Her lips had been tight and colorless. Oh, how he had loved it. And so had Camilla. It had been a perfect wedding, in her wonderfully twisted mind. It had reminded him more of Halloween or a film by Tim Burton. But he had let her have it her way, even though it was strange for him as well... because he loved her, and he wanted to make her happy.

Mikkel whistled and put more books on the shelf. Yes, there were many things the two of them didn't agree on, but their love was indisputable. They were going to be very happy in this cozy little house on this strange island. Mikkel just knew they would.

Mikkel looked inside the box to see how many were left.

It's almost empty. Just a few more books, and then you're done. Then, you can go to bed.

Mikkel whistled again, then reached down to grab the last books when he heard something. He looked up. It sounded like it came from the garden. Mikkel walked to the window, where he thought he had seen someone earlier.

Who was out there? A hobo looking through their rubbish? An animal of some sort? The house had been vacant for a long time. Who knew what creatures might be used to living out there, or even humans maybe?

Mikkel had lived in a city all of his life and wasn't used to the darkness or the wildlife on this island. He peeked out the window but couldn't see anything. Then he heard another sound. It sounded like the garden door slamming. There it was again. Was it the wind? It kept slamming.

Better go out and close it properly, he thought. *With that noise it makes, we'll never get any sleep tonight.*

Mikkel found his clogs and put them on. It wasn't too cold outside yet. Summer was almost over, and Mikkel didn't look forward to the fall. He hated the cold and had often dreamt about moving to a warmer country.

That's it. Next time Camilla demands a change, I'll tell her we'll move to Spain. If I can't grow old here in this house, then we might as well move far away. It would be good to get away from the old folks anyway.

He thought the thought but knew he would never follow through. It was too much trouble. How would he even get a job there?

Mikkel walked out the back door and into the garden, where the door was slamming again and again. He walked toward it, when suddenly, lights were turned on.

"What the...?" Mikkel said.

The big tree at the end of the garden was dressed in colorful Christmas lights. Mikkel couldn't recall the tree having lights when he was in the garden earlier today. He stared at it in disbelief, when suddenly, a big sign was folded out between two of the smaller trees.

WELCOME

Mikkel read it, not knowing what to make of it. Who had put it there? Who had put up the lights?

"SURPRISE!"

The voice came from behind the tree. A man came out from behind it. He was wearing sunglasses, even though the sun had set long ago.

"Excuse me?" Mikkel asked.

The man approached him. He was holding a bottle in his hand.

Mikkel found it all a little strange.

"Surprise!" he said again. He came up close to Mikkel. He was smiling. "It's a surprise party. To welcome you home."

Mikkel looked at the man. Was he for real? What the heck was this?

"I... but... but no one is here. It's just you?" he said, and scanned the garden to see if there could be others hiding behind the trees.

"I am your party," the man said, right before he slammed the bottle into Mikkel's head.

FORTY-SIX

AUGUST 2014

Victor woke up screaming that night. I ran to his room to help him calm down. His little body was shaking all over. His pj's were soaked in sweat.

"Mommy, Mommy, Mommy!"

"I'm here, Victor. I'm right here next to you. It was just a bad dream."

Victor lifted his head. I could tell he was looking at me, and I spotted his beautiful eyes between his curls.

"Scarecrows don't talk, Mommy. Scarecrows don't talk!"

I stared at my son. I didn't understand why he was saying this to me. Was it something from his dream? "No, of course they don't," I said. "Did you dream of scarecrows?"

"No, Mommy. No. Scarecrows don't talk. Scarecrows don't talk!"

He was yelling at me now. I hated that I didn't understand why he was saying this. I could tell it was very important to him.

"I'm sorry, sweetie. I don't understand... I don't know why you're telling me this."

"It's from that film again."

I turned my head and spotted Maya in the doorway. My heart dropped. "The same film?" I asked.

Maya nodded. She yawned.

"But... but why? Why is he saying this in the middle of the night?" My heart was racing, while Victor kept repeating the same sentence over and over again.

"Scarecrows don't talk. Scarecrows don't talk..."

It was about to drive me crazy. My heart was pounding in my chest. I had a feeling I had to react to this somehow. The last two times Victor had quoted this film, people had ended up dead. I couldn't just listen to this. I couldn't live with myself if someone was killed tonight, and I hadn't done anything about it. I had to do something.

But I had no idea what.

Then it struck me. The killer went after people who had just bought new houses!

"I'm going to do something about this, Victor, don't worry about it," I said, then stormed downstairs and grabbed my laptop. I opened my mailbox. I had subscribed to real estate listings a long time ago, while trying to find a house for my father when he wanted to move here. I received emails every day about new houses that had been placed on the market, and about houses that had just been sold. It was a long shot, but maybe...

I scrolled to the email I had received earlier that day, but there were no sold houses. I slammed my fist into the table. It had been a long shot, I knew, but somehow, I had hoped that I could...

If they moved in today, then they would have bought the house earlier. Maybe a couple of days ago, maybe even longer.

I searched my inbox and found all the emails I had received from the local real estate agent for the entire month. I started opening them, one after the other. It didn't take long before I found it. The latest sold house on the island was a small, two-bedroom, yellow brick house on the south side, in Sønderho.

The other killings had been here in Nordby. Would he move away from his comfort zone? I looked at my watch. It was almost midnight. It took about fifteen minutes to reach the other end of the island. It wasn't a very long drive. But, I did, of course, risk that he was attacking someone here in Nordby while I was gone. I scrolled through a few emails. No, there hadn't been any other houses sold on the island for weeks, it appeared.

It was a chance I had to take.

FORTY-SEVEN
AUGUST 2014

"Do I have to go?"

Sophia looked at me from the doorway. "I mean, I have the kids and everything."

"Isn't your mom still here?" I asked.

Sophia sighed. "It's late, and I'm really tired. Besides, it's just a hunch you have. Why do I have to be involved?"

"You're the only one I know who owns a gun," I said, and adjusted my shirt. I had put it on backward, getting dressed in a hurry, while telling Maya to look after her brother while I was gone.

"Hey, your boyfriend has one too. Can't you take him?" Sophia asked, while getting dressed very reluctantly.

"Hurry up," I said to her. "You know how things are with Morten. If I called him about this, he'd only think I was doing it to get close to him. Could you imagine if we drove down there and there's nothing? It would be so embarrassing. He'd think I made it all up. He'd think I was all pathetic and desperate."

"You *are* desperate," Sophia said.

"That might be, but I'm not pathetic. Now, grab that gun of yours, tell your mom you're leaving, and join me in the car."

"Yes, ma'am."

A minute later, we were both in the car, driving out of Nordby. I had my navigation direct us to the right address. My stomach was feeling all kinds of things... mostly nervousness, I think, and a little fear. No, that's a lie. It was a lot of fear.

"So, what you're telling me is that you believe the killer is going to kill these people, and we're heading there?"

"I just have to make sure these people are all right," I said. "I won't shut an eye till I'm sure they're fine."

"We're going to be on the news, you know that, don't you?" Sophia asked.

"I don't care if they think I'm weird. I just have to make sure."

I looked at the gun in Sophia's hands. I sure hoped it would do its job and protect us, once again, if it came down to it. But the fact was, neither of us was very handy with a gun. I had never shot one before. Sophia had hurt a guy once when he entered her house trying to attack her. But, even then, she had just shot him in the shoulder. Would that be enough protection? Neither of us really wanted to hold it, let alone shoot someone. I, for one, was terrified of killing someone.

"You have reached your destination," the navigation said.

I parked the car in front of the yellow brick house. The lights were on inside. Sophia looked at me. Then, she shrugged.

"Here goes nothing."

We got out of the car and started walking toward the house. I felt awkward, like it was all a dream.

We walked to the front door. I had no idea what to do. Should we knock? There were two cars parked on the street. A gray one farther down the road, and then a red one closer to the house. The couple's car was in the driveway.

I found a doorbell and rang it. No one answered. I grabbed the handle. It was locked. Then I knocked, in case the bell didn't work. Still no answer.

"There was light on in the garden," I said. "Let's go around and see if everything is all right."

Sophia hesitated as we reached the tall gate leading to the door. "I really don't want to spend the night in prison for breaking and entering," she said. "These people are going to think we're nuts, Emma. Is it really worth it?"

I grabbed the gun from her hand. It was heavier than I had imagined. Maybe it was the responsibility that came with it. "I'll go in alone, then."

"Be careful, Emma. Shoot first and ask questions afterward."

"Is that how you usually do it?" I asked.

"Just be careful. I'll never forgive myself if anything happens to you."

"Then you better pray that nothing does," I said, and grabbed the rusty handle on the old wooden gate. I pulled it open and stepped in.

I didn't even feel the gun drop to the ground, until I heard the sound.

After that, all I heard was my own scream.

FORTY-EIGHT
AUGUST 2014

The scream made Jesper Melander stop what he was doing. From inside the bedroom, he had heard the doorbell, then the knock, but figured that whomever it was would go away eventually when no one answered the door.

But, they hadn't. They had walked into the garden and seen it. Seen his work.

But it's not done yet!

Jesper growled angrily. The girl on the bed was moaning. He had knocked her out with the metal rod that was now on the floor with her blood on it, but he hadn't killed her... not yet. First, he wanted to undress her and give her his present.

He had it in his bag right next to him.

Jesper sprang for the window and spotted a woman standing in the garden. He knew her. He knew who she was. She was holding a hand to her face and screaming. On the ground next to her lay something.

A gun.

Another woman came storming through the gate. Now, she saw his unfinished work as well and started screaming too. Jesper growled, then cursed. Why were they destroying everything for him? The whole plan, the work of art he was making in the garden.

Think fast, Jesper. Think fast!

The only way out, as he saw it, was to walk down there and attack the two women, kill them, and put them up on a pole next to the husband.

But they might fight; they might use the gun.

Jesper was terrified of guns. There weren't many things that scared him, but guns did. Especially in the hands of unpredictable people.

Someone might have heard them scream. Someone might have heard them. The place will be crowded in just a few moments. It's time to go. Time to run for it.

Jesper glanced at the beautiful girl on the bed. She was still moaning in pain. He felt so drawn to her at this moment. He enjoyed watching people in pain. It was his favorite part of it all. Now, it had all fallen apart.

Should I just kill her? Stab her right here?

No. There wasn't enough time. He wanted her awake when he stabbed her. That was his favorite part of the killings.

There's no time, you fool. Do it quick. Then get out of here!

Jesper found the knife and walked over to the woman. He lifted the knife into the air and closed his eyes. Oh, the smell of a fresh kill. He would enjoy it, make the best of it, even if she wasn't awake to see how her life ended.

It was still worth it.

Just as Jesper was about to plunge the knife into the woman's chest, he heard feet coming up the stairs.

They're here. They've come into the house!

He heard fumbling at the door, someone trying to open it, but he had locked it so she wouldn't escape in case she woke up. Then someone yelled.

"Hello?"

Jesper smiled. *Fools.* "Hello?" he yelled back.

"Who's in there?" the female voice yelled back.

"Pay no attention to the man behind the curtain," Jesper said, making his voice sound light, like a female. Jesper giggled. He had always been excellent at making voices. For a while, growing up, he had thought that was what he was going to do for a living... be a comedian who did impressions. But the chance never quite presented itself to him.

Besides, he liked this better.

"What?"

Jesper scanned the room. There were no other ways out.

What are you going to do?

Jesper laughed a madman's laughter. This had turned out to be even more fun that he had ever dared to anticipate. So much more fun.

"Are you all right in there?" I yelled through the door, the gun shaking between my hands. The poor woman in there had no idea what had happened to her husband. Or maybe she did and had gone into shock. She didn't sound like she was in her right mind. What was that about a man and a curtain? I didn't understand. I was still shivering from what I had seen in the garden.

"Yes, yes, fine," she answered.

She sounded strange, I thought. And why wasn't she asking me who I was and what I was doing in her house? Something was definitely off.

"Something terrible happened," Sophia said. "I've called the police. Whatever you do, don't look out the window. Please unlock the door so we can help you."

"I'm afraid I can't," the voice replied. "The lock is broken."

I looked at Sophia, who shook her head. This was too weird. "Something is wrong here," I whispered to Sophia.

"Her voice sounds really strange," Sophia whispered back. "You think the killer is in there?" Sophia's voice was trembling.

I shrugged. "Maybe," I whispered back. "Maybe he has

someone in there with him. Maybe he's going to kill her. I'm going to kick the door in now, and then I'll use your method."

"My what?" Sophia asked.

"Shoot first and ask questions later."

I lifted my leg and kicked the door. I broke a giant hole in it, then kicked it again and got it open. Just as we walked into the room, we heard a loud crash, the sound of glass breaking.

"The window," I yelled.

I rushed toward it, just in time to see the killer slide across the roof and jump onto the branch of the big tree in the garden.

"Stop or I'll shoot!" I yelled after him, but he had already reached the ground and started running. When he reached the small red car and was about to get into it, he suddenly stopped. He turned his head and looked directly at me for just a second before he jumped inside the small red car and drove off.

"Shoot! He's getting away!" Sophia yelled.

"It's too late. He's gone," I said.

I heard moaning behind me and turned. A naked woman was on the bed, her arms and legs tied down. I ran to her. She had blood on her face.

"Are you all right?" I asked, while untying her arms and legs. In the distance, I could hear the siren from the island's only police car. I had asked Sophia to call for help, to avoid any confusion in case it was Morten who picked up the phone at the police station.

The woman groaned again. She was trying to open her eyes and lift her head, but it was too painful. At least she was alive. That was more than I could say for her poor husband in the garden. I still shivered when I thought about him. His dead body had been strapped onto a pole and placed in the middle of the garden. It made him look like a scarecrow.

Scarecrows don't talk. Of course.

I couldn't get the pictures out of my head... the head hanging lifeless from his neck, his chin touching his chest, his lifeless eyes staring into the darkness, the blood running from his wounds in the chest and leg. The killer seemed to have gutted his leg open, and I wondered if he had removed anything this time. The brain and the heart seemed both untouched.

I felt so confused. What was this all about? What was it with this killer's obsession with *The Wizard of Oz*? Who was he killing over and over again in his mind?

Voices came from downstairs; I could tell they belonged to Morten and Dr. Williamsen.

"Up here," Sophia yelled.

The woman was awake. She was blinking her eyes. "Where... where am I?" she asked.

"Shh. Don't get up." I spotted the metal rod on the floor. It had blood smeared on it. "You were hit on the head. Just stay still till the doctor comes. The police are on their way as well," I said. "Rest your head."

"Wh...?" The woman was overwhelmed with pain and didn't try to speak anymore.

I spotted a black sports bag next to the metal rod. It was open. I walked to it and looked inside. Then I gasped.

Sophia looked at me. "What?" she asked. "Is it the killer's?"

I stepped aside, so Sophia could take a look. She gasped as well. "The shoes. The ruby red slippers! He was going to put them on her, wasn't he?"

I nodded. "I think he was. We interrupted him and made him run."

"We saved her life?"

"I think we came just in time."

"Emma? What happened? Are you both all right?" Morten stormed in.

He stared intensely at me.

My heart started beating fast. It had been almost four weeks since he left me in my kitchen. I had no idea what to say to him. I just shook my head. "We're fine, I guess."

"This girl needs medical attention," Sophia said.

"What happened to her?" Dr. Williamsen asked.

"She was struck with that metal rod over there. Whoever did it, jumped through the window and disappeared in a small red car," I said. Then, I paused and took a deep breath.

"Her husband... is in the garden."

FIFTY

AUGUST 2014

Jesper Melander was washing his hands, rubbing them aggressively with soap. He was growling and groaning in anger.

How could it have gone so wrong?

He thought back to what had happened, while the blood from his fingers and arms turned the sink red. He was making a horrible mess. Jesper looked at himself in the mirror and tried to wash the bloodstains off of his cheeks.

You should have killed her while you had the chance, you fool. You should have killed them all... the two women as well.

Why hadn't he? Why hadn't he just killed them all? Instead, he had hesitated. He had shown weakness. He had panicked.

Carefully, he took off his shirt. It was filled with small pieces of glass from when he jumped through the window. It was lucky that he was so agile. All the workouts over the last few years had finally paid off. He was quite impressed with himself... to think that he had managed to climb over the rooftop and jump to the tree, then crawl down and jump to the ground. They didn't stand a chance. They would never catch him.

Jesper laughed at his own reflection.

Don't they know they'll never catch me, those fools? They have no idea who they're dealing with. They'll never find me.

But it had been close this time. Too close. That couldn't happen again. He would have to make sure of that.

Jesper had decided to change his plans slightly. He had to get rid of that woman. She had seen him. He was certain she had. Just as he had jumped into the car, he had turned his head and looked back. He had seen her standing in the window, looking at him. She knew too much. Why was she even there? Why was she knocking on the door this late at night? Were they neighbors? No. Jesper knew he had seen the woman in the window somewhere before. He had seen that face, those chubby cheeks, and annoying face before. But where?

He went to his office to look at the bookshelf. He ran his fingers over the back of his many books, then paused and took one out. He looked at the picture inside the flap. There she was. Looking right back at him, smiling like she knew his dirty little secret.

So you want to play ball, huh, Emma Frost?

Jesper closed the book with a slam, then threw it on the desk. He snorted in anger. She annoyed him immensely. He couldn't stand the fact that she was the reason why he hadn't succeeded in completing this kill, this piece of art. And, on top of it, he had lost the shoes. He'd had to leave the bag with the shoes behind, and he had never managed to put them on her feet. Jesper growled again, then grabbed the many listings of homes for sale on the island and ripped them apart. He threw the pieces on the floor and stomped on them in anger.

Jesper took a deep breath and leaned back his head, trying to calm himself down. This was not the time to lose control. It was all about staying on top of things. And he was always a step ahead, wasn't he? Yes, he had been so far. And this Emma Frost had no idea who she was dealing with. Besides, he had managed to finish the man. It was a stunning success... hanging him up him like a scarecrow in the garden. Jesper was impressed with his own ingenuity. It was quite clever, wasn't it? It would definitely make the newspapers in the morning.

Another cruel idea was slowly shaping in the mind of Jesper Melander. An idea so brutal, it caused him to smile at the very thought of it. Jesper rushed into the garage and searched through his mess. He pulled out a red gas can. It was heavy. He looked at it with delight. Then, he giggled at his own creativity.

Well, my little pretty, I can cause accidents too!

FIFTY-ONE

AUGUST 2014

The weekend passed and Monday came. I was still shaken up pretty badly about what had happened in Sønderho. I hadn't slept much since. I kept seeing the man in the garden, hanging from the pole, every time I closed my eyes. It freaked me out.

Every minute of my waking hours, I fought the urge to call Morten and ask him if they knew anything more about this killer, and if they were anywhere near finding him, but I was afraid he would think I was using the case as an excuse to talk to him, which might be partly true as well. I didn't want him to think I was as desperate as I felt.

The fact was, we hadn't spoken for four weeks now, except for the hour he spent with me on Friday night, writing down my testimony about what had happened when we arrived at the house. I had given him my description of the killer the way I saw him right before he jumped inside the red car. But, the fact was, I didn't see him very well in the darkness, and the little I saw from the light of the streetlamps on his face wasn't really useful. Morten had been very professional when interviewing me, and that hurt like crazy. He hadn't said a word about us or anything. He asked if I was all right. That was all. Not a hug, not a comforting word of any kind. I couldn't believe he could, all of a sudden, turn this cold. It almost made me cry just thinking about it.

I guess we were definitively over.

I had no idea what had happened to the woman on the bed, but assumed she had been airlifted to the mainland and was safe in the hospital. But, again, I didn't know, because I didn't want to call Morten. The newspapers said she was still in intensive care and that she had suffered a severe blow to the head.

Sophia came over and sat in my kitchen after lunch. She looked as bad as I felt inside.

"What? No cake or buns? You're not baking today?" she asked.

I poured her a cup of coffee.

"I'm not really in the mood," I said. I smiled awkwardly. The fact was, I had been in a baking frenzy all weekend and had just finished the rest of the carrot cake from the day before by myself. I was too embarrassed to tell Sophia, but I hadn't stopped eating all weekend. It was the only thing that kept me from thinking about the killings and about Morten.

"That's not like you," she said.

I sat with my cup between my hands and stared into the black coffee. Images of the woman on the bed flickered before my eyes.

"Can't blame you," Sophia continued. "I'm still freaking out as well.

Did you hear the latest?"

"No, what?"

"I read it in the newspaper this morning, but apparently the killer cut something out of the husband."

"I had a feeling he might have," I said. My heart started pounding. "What was it this time? The heart, the brain again?"

She shook her head. "No, it was way weirder than that. It was a nerve or something. Something that starts with an s."

I grabbed my laptop and found the article online in today's newspaper. I had stayed offline all morning, trying to keep my thoughts in other places.

"It's called the sciatic nerve," I said.

"What's that?"

I googled it. "Apparently it's the longest and widest single nerve in the human body. It goes from the top of the leg to the foot."

I looked at Sophia. She made a grimace. "Why on earth...?

"What's going on here?" I asked and leaned back. "What is this guy up to?"

"First he takes the heart, then the brain, and now a... a nerve from someone?"

"The heart, the brain, the nerve, where have I heard that before?" I stared at Sophia while it all came to me. "The heart, the brain, the nerve," I repeated over and over again, slowly remembering the song. I googled it and found the lyrics. Then I started singing.

Sophia jumped in.

I stared at Sophia, while we both sang the last sentence of the song in unison.

FIFTY-TWO

AUGUST 2014

"What do you make of it?"

Sophia looked agitated. She sipped her coffee, while looking at me like she expected me to know everything.

"He's obsessed with the film," I said. "Some obsession."

"Pretty creepy," I said, and sipped my coffee, while wondering what we could use this for. These were all the things the Scarecrow, the Tin Man, the Cowardly Lion, and Dorothy wanted to get from the Wizard of Oz. The Scarecrow needed a brain, the Tin Man needed a heart, and the Cowardly Lion needed courage, the nerve. So the killer collected all these things. Did that mean he was done?

"He still hasn't gotten what Dorothy wanted," I said.

"What?" Sophia asked. She looked confused.

"He has all the things the others wanted, the heart, the brain, the nerve, but he hasn't gotten what Dorothy wanted yet."

"And what was that?"

"A home. She wanted to go home."

Sophia scoffed. "So, you think he'll steal someone's house next?"

"Maybe. Who knows what he'll come up with?"

There was a fumbling by the front door, and I heard Maya enter. She stuck her face through the door to the kitchen.

"Hi," she yelled.

"Hi, sweetie. How was your day? Do you want something to eat?"

"No, I have homework. Maybe later."

Then she left.

"I'd better get back," Sophia said. She finished her coffee. "My kids will start pouring in as well in a few minutes."

I gave her a hug. "See you later."

A few minutes passed before Victor came through the door. As usual, he stormed into the kitchen and sat in his chair, waiting for his food to magically appear.

So, I toasted some bread and served it with jam on it. He hadn't slept well lately either and looked pale.

"So, how have you been, buddy?" I asked. "Is school getting better?"

He didn't answer. He stared at the table while chewing. Small talk didn't interest him. But, I figured that because he didn't say anything, he'd had a good day. I reached into my pocket and pulled something out and placed it on the table in front of him.

"I found this rock this morning while taking my walk on the beach. You think you'd like it?" I asked.

Finally, he lifted his eyes. He stared at the yellow rock. He had been into rocks a lot lately. Rocks and trees were his entire life.

He grabbed it and looked at it in the light. I felt really proud, seeing the smile on his face. He felt it in his hand, then hit it against his front tooth.

"It's amber, Mom."

"Really? Well, I had a feeling you would know what it was. It's yours if you want it."

Victor looked at me and smiled. "Thanks."

My heart skipped a beat. It was so rare that I got to make my son happy. It felt so good, the few times I succeeded.

"It's going in my collection," he said and stood up, then stormed through the house. I heard the door to the garden slam and knew he would be busy for the next several hours. It made me happy to know he was happy out there with his rocks and trees.

I had just finished cleaning up his food when Dr. Sonnichsen arrived. I let her in and called for Maya, who ran down the stairs. She was always looking forward to the sessions with Dr. Sonnichsen, and especially today, because it had been the weekend.

They went into the living room to do their thing, and I returned to the kitchen and started preparing dinner. I looked at my laptop while peeling potatoes. I hadn't gotten much work done today either and was starting to get stressed out about this book. All I needed was to edit two chapters, but somehow, I couldn't find the energy to do it. I kept wondering about the strange Wizard of Oz killer. Then, I thought about Morten, who was all alone trying to crack the case. I knew he was probably very frustrated by now.

Once I was done with the potatoes, I turned on the small TV in my kitchen and started watching the news. I turned up the volume as the report came to the killings on Fanoe island. Apparently, the woman had woken up, and they had made a police sketch of the killer from her memory. They showed the drawings and told the viewers to contact the local police if they saw this man.

"He is considered very dangerous, so do not approach him if you see him," the anchor said insistently.

I looked the drawing up on the TV station's website and printed it out. I stared at it for a little while. It was very close to what I believed he looked like... the long hair in a ponytail, the goatee, the sunglasses covering his eyes. Yes, that was exactly the man I had seen. In the description, it said he was wearing a leather vest and jeans.

I couldn't remember that. But I did remember the ponytail and sunglasses. I had told Morten about those two things as well when I had given my description.

I sat by my computer for a little while, staring at the picture, and couldn't figure out where I had seen him before. There was something familiar about him. Was he some sort of celebrity?

I put the picture down and returned to my Danish meatballs, frikadeller. I turned them in the pan and turned the heat down a little so they wouldn't burn. Dr. Sonnichsen came into the kitchen.

"We're done for the day," she said. "Just wanted to let you know, we started a new program, and Maya is responding very positively to it. I'm starting to get my hopes up."

My heart dropped. Such a relief. "I'm so glad to hear that," I said. "You have no idea..."

"What's this?" Dr. Sonnichsen suddenly said and picked up the police sketch from the kitchen table.

"Ah, it's just a sketch of the guy who possibly killed our neighbors and two other couples."

"Ah, him. Well, good thing that they now have a drawing. He looks awfully familiar, though, don't you think?"

"Yes! Thank you," I said, and set the spatula down. I approached the doctor and looked at the picture with her. "I do think he looks very familiar. But I can't remember where I've seen him before. Do you know?"

She looked pensive. "He kind of looks like that guy who runs those self-help classes. You know, where a man can learn how to become a man again."

"Ah, yeah," I exclaimed. "That's it. He looks just like that annoying guy who takes men into the woods to have them run around naked until they feel comfortable with their bodies again. Yes, that's right. It does look like him. A lot."

"He has a place here on the island where he lives and has the classes. It's a farm, I believe. It caused a lot of turmoil when he moved there, I remember. I lived in Copenhagen then, but I clearly remember the stories. Wasn't he accused of killing his ex-girlfriend and her sons once?" Dr. Sonnichsen asked.

"Oh, yeah, that's right. Now I remember him. And of killing his mother, many years back. But he was acquitted of all of them, as far as I remember. And he got married and changed his name, so no one would know who he was, which was odd because the name change was all over the newspapers. What was the new name again?"

"Jesper Melander."

FIFTY-THREE

AUGUST 2014

I couldn't stop thinking about what Dr. Sonnichsen said for the rest of the evening. We had dinner and I talked on the phone with my dad. He and my mom were heading back to the island tomorrow, they told me.

After getting the kids to bed, I sat down with my computer and started researching Jesper Melander.

There was a lot written about him and his so-called male classes. According to the articles I found, Jesper Melander was originally called Bjarke Lund, but he changed his name after the media had named him the killer of the century. It was understandable enough that he wanted to start over after being acquitted, I thought.

Apparently, he had gotten married while still in prison, and as soon as he was freed, he had moved in with her, but the press still wouldn't leave them alone. And neither would the people. No matter where the woman went, people would tell her how stupid she was for marrying a killer.

So, they moved to the countryside. In her last interview I could find, the woman, whose name was Louise Melander, told the journalist that they were going to move away from everything to be able to live in peace.

But the husband had not kept his face out of the newspapers. He had gotten an education as a therapist, and a few years later, he had started what he called The Caveman School. In several articles, they wrote about how men paid a lot of money to be able to act like wild savages. They would run around the forests, naked, and yell and scream like cave dwellers.

"We're taking back our manhood," Jesper Melander said in one article. "And women are going to learn to love it."

There were pictures of men in mud fights, men fighting wearing sumo suits, and swinging from ropes between the trees, while apparently screaming like Tarzan. There were pictures of men being baptized in beer, fighting with clubs, and even one of a man lying on top of a car, while Jesper Melander drove through the marshland trying to get him to fall off.

It was so ridiculous I had to laugh. Who would pay money for such a class? Well, apparently, it had a lot of success, according to the articles, and Jesper Melander had become quite wealthy over the years, since his release from prison in 2010.

I leaned back in my chair and wondered about this guy. If I could see that it was him in the drawing, then the police had to be able to see it as well, didn't they? Or maybe not.

I searched a little more and found an old clip from an interview he had done, back when he was first accused of killing his mother. I clicked it and started watching. As I did, my heart started racing. The guy had painted his face green, like the Wicked Witch of the West!

That was enough proof for me. This guy was obviously into *The Wizard of Oz*, just like our killer. This couldn't be a coincidence.

It was time to follow the urge and call Morten.

My hands were shaking, as I found his number and pressed the button.

"Hello, Morten? Hi, it's Emma."

A long devastating silence broke out.

Oh no! Why did I do this? Why did I call him? He hates me, doesn't he?

"Emma!"

He sounds happy. Why does he sound happy?

"How are you? I've been thinking about you since Friday night. Are you all right?"

I exhaled in relief. He wasn't mad that I called. I felt tears pressing from behind my eyes.

"I... I'm okay, I guess. It hasn't been fun, I'll tell you that much."

"I know, Emma. I'm so sorry for... well, for everything. I haven't been myself lately." He sighed before he continued. "I... since I saw you Friday, I haven't been able to stop thinking about you. I realized how much I've missed you."

"I've missed you too." It was getting harder to hold back the tears now, but I fought with everything I had to do it anyway. He wasn't going to make me cry. I was angry with him.

"So, what's up?" he asked. "Why did you call?"

"I saw the sketch on TV and printed it out. I was wondering if you recognized him as well." I said, swallowing my pride. I wanted so badly to ask him to come over... to come and stay the night. Tell him I missed his arms, that I would forgive him for walking out on me, for not making me the first priority in his life.

"Yes. I know," he said with a heavy voice. "It looks a lot like Jesper Melander, doesn't it?"

"Oh, good. You see it as well. So, what will happen next?"

"He is definitely our main suspect right now, but so far, all we have is the drawing. I went out there today and questioned him and he had alibis for every killing. They were all women whom he had slept with on the nights of the killings."

I was surprised to hear that. "So, I take it you couldn't take him in?"

"Nope. But I'm working on it. Believe me. We've taken a DNA sample, and we're running it against what we have from the scene."

"You found DNA on the scene?" I asked hopefully.

"We found a hair that didn't belong to any of the victims, yes. On the bed in the house where he struck on Friday. As soon as we have the result on that one and it proves positive, we'll take him in. Don't you worry about that."

"I guess I won't then. I'm so glad you've cracked the case," I said.

"I wouldn't say I cracked it. It's still too early to celebrate, but at least we're heading somewhere," he said.

An awkward silence broke out between us again. I thought of a thousand things to say, but they all seemed so dull and stupid.

"So, how have you been?" I asked, fearing he would hang up if I didn't say anything.

"Busy. And you?"

"Busy too. Trying to finish my book. It's taking a lot longer than I expected it to."

"It always does," he said, distracted.

Silence again. Should I just say goodbye and hang up? It was beginning to feel painful. But I wasn't ready to let go of him yet. I had missed talking to him so terribly, and now I finally had the chance.

"So..." he said. "I should..." Then he paused.

Oh, that dreadful silence between us. How had it come to this? We used to talk about everything!

That's when it happened. The thing I didn't want to

happen. I said the only thing I had promised myself I wasn't going to say. "I still love you, you know."

I don't know how it happened. I just blurted it out. I had kept silent for so long. I guess I just wanted to say it.

I closed my eyes and wished I could take it back.

Oh, my. He's wondering what to say next without hurting me. Why did I call him? Why? He was supposed to call me and tell me how much he missed me. Why did I call him?

I heard a sigh from the other end. It wasn't good. It was deep and troubled.

"I…"

He was looking for the words. I wondered if I should just hang up right away. Save myself the embarrassment.

"I still love you too," he said.

My heart stopped. I couldn't believe what he was saying. I thought he had moved on. What did this mean?

"It's just… well, it's a little complicated right now," he said, speaking in a low voice.

Who was in the room next to him that he didn't want to hear him say these words to me? Was he with another woman? What was going on?

"Is there someone else?" I asked, my voice breaking.

"No. No. Oh, no, Emma. Let me just take this in the other room." I heard him open a door, then close it again before he returned. "It's Jytte. She's freaking out about us. She says she'll move into her own place if I keep seeing you. I don't know what to do. I'm just trying to figure everything out, Emma. That's all. I need a little time."

"Time for what? She's seventeen, Morten. Is she supposed to control everything in your life forever? So what if she threatens to move away from home? She'll never do it, Morten. She's in school. She doesn't have that kind of money."

"I know. I'm just afraid she might do something stupid and get herself in trouble, okay?"

Part of me understood, but another part wanted him to tell her she was acting like a baby and that she needed to grow up. But the fact was, she wasn't my daughter, and I had no say in this. If he needed time to deal with her, then I would give him just that.

"You know what? Take all the time you need," I said, feeling all of a sudden convinced there was only one right solution to this. There was only one way I could deal with this without losing myself in the process.

"But don't expect me to wait for you. I'm done, Morten. This time, I'm the one who wants out."

I hung up with my heart pumping in my throat. I was sad, on the verge of devastation, but it had been a long time since something had felt this right.

FIFTY-FOUR

AUGUST 2014

Another week passed. Every day, I searched eagerly through the newspapers to see if there was any news of Jesper Melander being arrested. But still there was nothing. It irritated me immensely.

Who knew what atrocities the guy was up to while we were waiting? Was he planning on killing another couple? Had he already done it, but no one had found them yet?

My thoughts drove me crazy. There were days I could hardly think of anything else. I studied the housing market closely, and every day, I went through all my emails with my heart pounding, fearing to find that another house had been sold on the island.

Luckily, it hadn't happened yet.

I looked up everything I could about Jesper Melander and his previous life as Bjarke Lund, and the more I did, the more convinced I became that he had to be the killer. In my opinion, he fit the profile, and maybe cleverer than any killer I had encountered. Somehow, he had managed to get out of every kill he had committed. I just hadn't the faintest idea how.

Sophia was with me on my search. She wanted to nail the

guy as much as I did. I guess being the first to see someone who was killed made us feel like we owed it to them to get revenge for them. That was how I felt, after all. I felt like I had to help the poor people who couldn't act for themselves anymore, and make sure the villain got what he deserved.

On a positive note, Maya was getting a lot better. Every day, I saw improvement in her, and every day, I thanked Dr. Sonnichsen for working with her. I couldn't remember being this grateful to a stranger in my life before. It was such a blessing, and I knew it was one I risked losing any day. I had no idea if the region would take her away again sometime soon. Dr. Sonnichsen kept telling me she wasn't going anywhere, but I wasn't convinced. It was very expensive for the region to have someone like Dr. Sonnichsen work with only one child. So, I tried to enjoy her while I could, and make the most of her for the one hour a day she was here.

On the following Monday, I lost my patience and hacked my way into the police database. To my surprise, I found nothing new. It seemed that they had hardly worked on the case at all. The forensics team had finished their report on Mikkel Hermansen, the last victim. But there was nothing about the hair that Morten had talked about. Did it take that long to analyze it? Morten had told me Jesper Melander had agreed to let them take a sample from him to compare with, so I was surprised to see that nothing had come of it yet.

Maybe I was just being too impatient. I simply couldn't understand why they didn't just arrest the guy.

Sophia laughed at me when she came over for coffee a little later in the morning. She had Mondays off and was supposed to use them to clean her house, but rarely made it that far, as she was always hanging out at my place. I loved it when she stopped by, and I always made sure to have enough coffee in the pot.

"You can't just arrest a guy like Jesper Melander," she said. "He plays with the big boys now. They all attend his classes...

that he calls therapy lessons. But they've all been there, all the big businesspeople in Denmark. They love him. Even some of the royal family attended one of his classes once. It's true. They all like that stuff. He tells it as it is, you know. Makes them proud to be men. He tells women to get back in the kitchen and let the man be the man and provide for them."

"I hate him already," I said.

"He's just provoking, that's all. Gives him lots of business to say things like that."

"Yeah, I know. But it makes me so angry when people say stuff like that."

"That's why he does it. He says what the CEOs wish they could say out loud." Sophia grinned.

I could tell an idea was shaping in her head.

"We should pay him a visit. Just to check him out."

FIFTY-FIVE
AUGUST 2014

It was the worst idea ever. Still I couldn't deny the fact that I was curious as hell. And the police didn't seem to be doing anything. They had interviewed the guy, and he had told them his alibis and whereabouts during the killings.

I didn't believe any of it. It was very frustrating, knowing what he was capable of, to have him on the loose like this. And Sophia was right. They couldn't just arrest him if they didn't have hard evidence. The fact that he looked like the guy in the drawing wasn't quite enough.

I stared at Sophia across from me. I wondered about Morten and what he had been doing this last week. I couldn't believe he had nothing to link the guy to the killings.

"He's killed five people," Sophia. "I don't think we should. It's way too dangerous."

Sophia shrugged. "Maybe you're right. I just thought that maybe if you were face-to-face with him, then maybe you could be sure it was, in fact, him you saw run from the house that night. Then you could tell the police that you're certain it was him."

"I'm not sure it's enough," I said. "They need more evidence to place him there."

"We could go there and pretend to be journalists. Tell him we wanted to do an interview with him. He loves that stuff. Maybe we could snoop around a little. See if we could find a pair of ruby red slippers or something? Then call the police and let them know where to find it."

"That's not an awful idea," I said. "But what if he recognizes me?"

"You think he saw you that night?"

I shrugged and sipped my coffee. I felt a tickling sensation in my stomach. I had been passive for too long now. I really needed to do something about this guy. I felt like, if I didn't, then no one would. The police didn't have the capacity to investigate this properly. And, even if they did, they might be too late. This guy could kill a lot of people while we waited for them to build a case.

"I don't know. It was dark. He was under the streetlamp, so that's why I could see him. I don't know how much he was able to see from where he was standing. I doubt it if he could see anything at all."

Sophia smiled. "We could disguise you. You can borrow one of my mom's wigs."

"Those awful red-haired ones?" I said.

Sophia's mom's hair had become very thin with age, so she insisted on wearing these horrible wigs that didn't fit her very well. Still, it could work, I thought. Maybe if I added glasses? I had a pair in my wardrobe. Yes, that might just work. The guy had, after all, only seen me from very far away and it was dark. I wasn't even certain he had looked at me.

I tapped my fingers on the kitchen table. It was still early in the day. We had plenty of time to go there and come back before the kids returned from school. All I wanted was to get into his house for a little while and take a peek. And maybe talk to the guy. Pretending to interview him wasn't a bad idea. I was quite surprised by Sophia's ingenuity.

"I'll bring my gun, if that makes you feel any better," Sophia said.

"I can't just sit here and do nothing, while he's planning to kill more people. They might have children the next time. I've got to at least do something. I'm in," I said.

Sophia laughed. She got up and looked at me. "Great. I'll get the wig, and we'll have you disguised beyond recognition in no time." She paused. Then, she smiled, satisfied. "Oh, my. How exciting. I feel like Thelma and Louise. Or, uh, Miss Marple or something."

Now it was my turn to laugh.

FIFTY-SIX
AUGUST 2014

We didn't want him to be prepared for us, so we didn't call ahead to let him know we were coming. Instead, we took a chance and just drove there and knocked on the door.

It was almost noon when we drove up the long driveway toward the old farm. The gravel crunched underneath the wheels of my car. I was nervous, and there were times when I thought about turning around and going back.

I parked the car in front of the main building, looked at myself in the mirror, and made sure the wig was on right.

I didn't look too bad, I thought. It was believable that this could actually be my hair and glasses. But, most important of all, there was no chance he would ever recognize me. Even if he knew who I was or had read my books. I looked very different.

To my surprise, he opened the door himself... wearing nothing but his birthday suit.

I blushed and looked at Sophia. She sounded bewildered as she spoke.

"Mr. Melander?"

He smiled and leaned on the door, like it was the most

natural thing in the world, him being naked in front of two female strangers.

Then, he shook his head. "Not anymore," he said.

"Excuse me?" Sophia asked.

He could tell we were taken aback by his nakedness and seemed to enjoy it. I tried hard to look anywhere but down there...

"I changed it," he said. "A couple of months ago. I was sick and tired of it. I needed a change. I'm Steffen Carlsen now. Who are you?"

"I'm Laura Bo and this is Mille Bille, my photographer," Sophia said. I held the camera between my hands, so he could see it.

"We're from the *Zeeland Times*," Sophia continued.

Steffen Carlsen looked interested. I wanted to punch that smug look off of his face. It annoyed me already.

"Oh, are you now?" he asked.

"Yes," Sophia said. "We're covering the recent killings on the island and thought of asking for your expert analysis of this killer, your professional opinion as a therapist, and, well, as someone who knows men very well."

Steffen Carlsen chuckled, while scrutinizing me. It made me highly uncomfortable. "And don't journalists call in advance anymore?"

"We were in the area," I took over. "To be honest, we didn't think of you until we drove by out here and both agreed it could be interesting to hear your opinion on the murders that everyone is talking about."

I could tell he bought it. I couldn't tell if it was because he was flattered, or if he liked the fact that everybody was talking about his killings. Steffen Carlsen smiled widely and opened the door completely.

"All right then. Any publicity is good publicity, I always say. I have plenty to say about this. Come on in."

My heart was pumping hard in my chest as I walked past him into his house. There was no doubt in my mind anymore. Standing in front of him in person made me certain. This was the guy I had seen that Friday night under the streetlamp. Now, all we had to do was find something to prove it.

As he slammed the door behind us and let us into his living room, I couldn't tell if we were the clever ones, or if we had just walked willingly into the lion's den.

I guess I was about to find out.

FIFTY-SEVEN
AUGUST 2014

"You know, I have to say, this is the first time anyone has ever come to me to ask for an expert statement about a killer," Steffen Carlsen said, and showed us to the couches.

He sat down in a chair in front of us, not making any attempt to cover himself up. I got the feeling he was enjoying seeing our facial expressions.

"Well, you are an expert on the subject," Sophia said with a smirk.

"That I am. Not only because of my background in therapy, but also because I have spent time in prison with them. And, I'll tell you, they're not as bad as you like to make them out in the media. Most often, they suffer from long-term hurt and terrible childhoods. It's not just a cliché. It's a fact. Many of them are very sensitive creatures who never had anyone love them, but I tell you, love heals everything. That and sex," he took time to laugh at his own remark before he continued. "It was while I was in prison that I decided to become a therapist. I could tell there was a great need for someone like me. I just didn't have any idea how great the need actually was."

I grabbed the camera and started taking some photos while

he talked. He seemed to like the fact that I was looking at him through the lens. He smiled at the right time and looked into the camera like he was posing. He even took his penis in his hand and made that pose as well.

"That's not gonna make it in the newspaper," I said.

"I know," he laughed. "Just messing with you. It amuses me how frightened women are of the male sex organ."

"Does it now?" I said, trying hard to not get provoked by his remarks. I continued to take photos and tried to take some of the living room as well, looking through the lens, searching, scanning frantically for anything that could indicate he was actually the killer.

"Yes. It is interesting, don't you think? Our relationships with our sex organs. I have actually recently written a book about it. What startled me was when I realized that women completely ignore their vaginas. I studied hundreds of women for years, and came to the conclusion that, while men love their penises and often caress them in the shower, women choose to ignore their vaginas. That's too bad, don't you think? It's a shame. To men, the penis is the most important part of the body and they keep a close connection with it. I always tell my students that my cock is my god! I try to make them feel the same about theirs. I mean, why not? I worship mine. And so does my wife. She adores it. I kid you not. Every morning, I have her say good morning to it, and give it a good morning kiss. Just to acknowledge its importance in our marriage."

I felt nauseated listening to all this. I couldn't believe what he was saying. How pompous and self-indulged could a man be allowed to be? Did he say he had studied hundreds of women? Was he just being unfaithful to his wife on a regular basis and proud of it or what? All of his alibis had been with different women, Morten had told me. He made me sick... just from looking at him, sitting there flashing his penis at us, acting like we should worship it as much as he did.

He stared at me while I walked around in his living room with my camera. I felt his eyes on my body, on my behind when I turned the other way. He was scrutinizing me, observing me.

It made me very uncomfortable.

"So, these killings, huh?" he said. "Terrible story. But these acts, these killings... those poor families."

"So, what do you make of the killer? Who are we dealing with here, from what you know?" Sophia asked.

I lifted my head from the camera and looked at his face as he spoke. He didn't seem at all thrown off by the question. On the contrary. He was enjoying this, wasn't he? He liked this situation, the bastard. It made him feel on top. Us running to him for expertise. It made him feel strong.

Was that how it felt to kill those people, huh? Was it all just a power trip for you, you bastard?

FIFTY-EIGHT

AUGUST 2014

"It's what's inside the killer's head that we must look at, naturally," Steffen Carlsen said.

"Most killings are about sex or money or revenge. These are not. There might be a sexual aspect to it, the killer might get off by killing these people, but there is more to it than that."

"And what might that be?" Sophia asked. "What do you think this killer gets out of it?"

Steffen Carlsen threw out his hands. "I would say an act of cleansing. He is taking these people's lives at the moment they are starting them together... when they've just bought the house of their dreams, and everything is so pure and new. That's when he strikes and rips it apart. It's the beginning of a new life. And, I believe he takes something from them, right?"

The way he spoke sounded like he idolized the killer. I didn't care for that.

"It might be a sort of artwork in his mind, maybe like a hunting trophy; it seems to be almost ceremonial. The last victim was put on a pole to be displayed. Very ritualistic. It might even be religious."

It was bullshit. He was just talking, playing us. Had he seen through us, recognized me behind my disguise? Did he know we weren't really from the *Zeeland Times*? Or was this just the way he was?

"You seem to know a lot about these killings," Sophia continued.

"I read the newspaper, like everyone else," he answered.

"Do you know anything besides what has been in the newspapers?" Sophia asked.

Steffen Carlsen took a breath, looking like he was reflecting on the question. "No. I don't see how I could."

"Did you know any of the victims?"

He shook his head. I could tell he was wondering about the character of the questions. Sophia had to be careful now.

"I don't think I do. I don't socialize with people on this island a lot. They really don't want me here and made that clear in several open letters to the local newspaper and by protesting outside in the street once I moved here. It's quieter now, but they still tend to approach my wife and me when we go shopping. We stay away from the town for that same reason. I thought changing my name again might help, but I can't seem to escape my past, even though I was falsely accused. To most people, I'm still a murderer. I even think I might be in your eyes as well. You think I know this guy or something? That we all know each other and therefore I should have some sort of knowledge that no one else has? What? You think we speak over the phone? You think he calls me and brags to me? Is that it? Or is it because you think I did it? Please explain why you would ask these kinds of questions."

That shut Sophia up. She stared at him, and I could tell she was wondering what to do next. That was when I saw it. I had been looking at the many photographs on Steffen Carlsen's wall behind him. I lifted the camera and zoomed in. Then I took pictures of all of them. They all appeared to be women, but one of them struck me as someone I knew. Someone I had seen before.

I photographed it, then the other young women as well. I turned to face the TV, and walked a little in the other direction, while Sophia figured out the right response. I knew I had to act fast. We were running out of time and his patience. He seemed angry with us now.

"So, tell me, Miss Bo, can you explain to me why people picking fake names always make them sound either too phony or too common?"

I swallowed hard, and then took a couple more photos.

"I guess you know which category you and your little friend with the wig here belong to," he continued.

My jaw almost dropped. I looked at Sophia. Who had we been kidding? Well, not him, that was for sure. He had been on to us from the beginning. To our luck, at that same moment, the woman from the many articles I had read, his wife, who married him while he was still in prison, walked into the room. She wasn't very pretty. I remember thinking the same thing when looking at the pictures of her. And Steffen Carlsen was, undeniably, a good-looking guy... if you liked men with long hair and beards. But there was something about him that made me understand why women fell for him. He had a charm, a powerful way of owning the room. I could never fall for a chauvinistic, self-indulged pig like him, but I knew lots of women who could.

The woman entering the room seemed bigger, though, than the one I had seen in the newspapers. She had grown wider, more muscular. She actually came off a little manly to me.

"Louise!" Steffen exclaimed.

"Sorry," she said. "I didn't know you had company. I was just on my way to my CrossFit class."

Louise looked at us like she wanted her husband to present us. He didn't bother.

"They were just leaving," he said.

FIFTY-NINE

AUGUST 2014

She watched the two women get into their car and leave. Then, she pulled the curtain to cover up the window.

"Who were those two women, Bjarke?" she asked, as she walked back into the living room. She still called him by his birth name. That was the name of the man she had loved and married, and he could change it all he wanted to, but to her, he would always be the same.

Bjarke didn't answer, so she walked closer. "What did they want?" Louise could hear her voice shiver slightly. She still couldn't get used to all the women he brought home from time to time. She couldn't control her jealousy, even though it happened almost every week.

"Tell me, Bjarke. Who were they?" She grabbed his shoulder to make him look at her, but she shouldn't have done that.

As usual, it happened so fast she didn't see it coming. He hit her so hard, she flew across the room and landed on a dining room chair. Her face was burning, and she couldn't get up right away.

"Could you just stop talking for one moment, woman, and let a man think!" he yelled.

He always said things like that. He always told her to stay out of his affairs... to never ask questions. He would tell her she drove him to hit her.

It was all her fault. Louise had picked up CrossFit and had gotten stronger over the years, in the hope of being able to defend herself against his anger that she felt from the very first day he came to her flat when he was released from prison. She had worked on building her muscles for years, but he was still stronger than she was.

"Please... please, don't..." she said, while watching him walk closer to her.

"Don't what?" he growled.

"Don't hurt me again. I won't ask any more questions. I promise."

A series of blows rained down on her. Louise screamed. He grabbed her by the hair and pulled her up. Then he whispered, "You know you can scream all you want. No one will hear you. The farm is empty. We're in the middle of nowhere."

"I'm sorry, Bjarke," she pleaded. "I won't say any more. I won't even scream. Just let go of me. Just..."

Bjarke suddenly laughed. "You're not fooling me. I know you like it," he said. "You like the pain just as much as I like to see you in pain."

He was getting aroused now. His sex organ was getting hard. "No... no... Bjarke..."

He pulled her by the hair through the kitchen and down the stairs to the basement. She knew what would happen next.

"Please... not today, Bjarke. I promise I'll be good. I promise."

He flipped a switch and turned on the light. Louise hated this place more than anywhere in the world. Chains hung from the ceilings, and she remembered the time he had left her there for three days, only coming down to whip her every now and then and have sex with her while her arms were hurting from the chains. He had placed a sex swing in there that he placed her in every time he felt like it. There were ropes, shackles, straitjackets, cuffs, and worst of all, the bondage wheel that he was now strapping her onto.

"Please don't, Bjarke. I'll be good. I promise."

"Oh, you'll be good. I'll make sure of it," he said, and slapped her across the face as soon as she was strapped to the steel wheel.

Then, he reached over to the crafting table and grabbed the shoes. He put them on her feet, then grabbed the wheel and spun it. He stopped her as she was turning upside down, then forced his sex organ into her mouth. He pressed himself deep into her throat, till she could hardly breathe, while he looked at the shoes and screamed out into the room.

SIXTY
AUGUST 2014

"It is him and I can prove it!"

Sophia had hardly managed to knock on my door before I pulled it open and dragged her inside. It was the day after we visited the farm, and Sophia had been at work at the school.

"What?" she asked, surprised.

We went to the living room, where my computer was on the coffee table, the camera next to it.

"I've been going through the pictures all morning, and you won't believe what I found," I said.

We sat down, and I found the pictures. "I knew it was him when I laid my eyes on him, and now we have this to ring him up on." I opened two pictures and let her look.

"What am I looking at here?" Sophia asked. "She's a very pretty young woman, but...?"

"Don't you recognize her? It's Camilla Hermansen. Well, you've only seen her half dead, lying on the bed. Plus, it's at least five years old. She's a teenager."

"So, Jesper Melander, or Steffen Carlsen, or whatever his name is, knew her!" Sophia said.

"Yes, he did. I believe the wall is a wall of conquests he has made over the years. Girls he has been with."

"They are awfully lightly dressed," Sophia said.

"If you look at them, you'll see that some of them have whips in their hands and leather straps around their necks," I said, and showed her some of the pictures.

Sophia looked appalled.

"It would be like him to have a wall like that to brag about all his conquests," Sophia said. "I feel bad for that wife of his. Having to look at that every day. What a life."

I shrugged. "She chose it. She knew she married a nutjob. I'm more worried that he might kill her."

"So, now we know he knew one of the girls, what else?" she asked.

I clicked on another picture from the folder. "I had to zoom in a lot, but here it is. Look what film he watched recently."

Sophia studied the picture, showing an open DVD box. "*The Wizard of Oz*."

"Who owns that if they don't have any children?" I asked.

Sophia nodded pensively. "Only someone truly obsessed with the film, I guess."

"Like our killer. Add those two things to the mix, and the fact that I'm certain I saw him, I think there's at least enough to take him in for further questioning."

Sophia gave me a high five. "Guess it's time to call Morten, then."

I paused. Sophia saw it. She could tell by my face that I was having trouble calling him.

"You want me to do it?" she asked.

I didn't know. On the one hand, it would be great if I didn't have to call him; I would like to save myself from the embarrassment. I was still licking my wounds, trying to get over him. The last thing I needed right now was to have him back in my life, even if it was to nail a killer. On the other hand, he would know I had made Sophia call; she would have to tell him that I was a part of it all, and he would only think it was strange that I didn't call him myself. He might even get hurt or think I was childish for acting like this.

"I think I'd better do it myself," I said, and grabbed the phone. "But thanks."

"No problem. Good luck."

I called his phone, but he didn't answer. It made me angry. He always answered his phone. He was probably screening his calls. It could only be because he didn't want to talk to me. Who was being childish now, huh?

I called the police station instead, and Morten picked up.

"This is Emma. This is not a private call. I have something for you," I said, leaving no room for him to talk. "Two things. First, Jesper Melander, who now calls himself Steffen Carlsen, knew Camilla Hermansen. He has her picture on his wall in his living room. Second, he has *The Wizard of Oz* on DVD, and has been watching it recently. The empty cover was right next to his TV. Plus, I have now been face-to-face with him, and there's no doubt it was him I saw from the window as he jumped into a small red car. I will even agree to testify to that if you need it."

"I know, Emma. I know all of what you just told me."

"What?"

"We brought him in this morning. The hair found at the scene of crime matched his. He's going in for a lot of years. It's over, Emma. We got him."

SIXTY-ONE
AUGUST 2014

So, they had finally nailed him. I felt a glimpse of satisfaction, knowing he was behind bars and about to be put away for many years. There was something so deeply gratifying about this fact.

He was going to get what he deserved. Finally.

For a couple of days, I managed to let go of the case and take care of my family. I was licking my wounds too, after the breakup with Morten, but the more time that passed, the more I became certain it had been the right thing to do. I couldn't stay in a relationship where I was a third wheel. I simply couldn't. I missed Morten every day, and especially at night, but I stood by my decision. It had to be this way.

Three days after the arrest, I invited my parents over for dinner and spent time with the people who mattered the most to me. My family.

Just as we had eaten the main course and my dad and I both leaned back in our chairs and opened the top button of our jeans, my phone rang.

A woman presented herself. "My name is Dina Wangede. I'm an attorney. I represent Steffen Carlsen."

My eyes grew wide. What was this? Why was she calling

me, of all people? If anything, I was only going to testify against him. I had no business talking to anyone who wanted to defend the bastard.

"Okay," I said, shaking my head in disbelief. "What can I do for you?"

"He wants to see you."

I burst into laughter. "Like that's ever going to happen."

"He said it was very urgent. He asked me to beg if I had to. He believes he has something important to tell you."

I shook my head with a grimace. Who did he think he was? Why would I want to visit him?

"Oh, yeah. And what might that be?" I asked.

"He wouldn't tell me, but he said to tell you that he would give you exclusive rights to tell his story."

I paused. This just got interesting. "Tell his story, huh? And he'll let me interview him and get all the details? I mean everything? He'll tell me everything, and be completely honest with me?"

"Yes. That's what he said. It's quite the deal, Mrs. Frost."

"Tell him I'll stop by tomorrow."

I hung up with a smile across my lips. It wasn't the prospect of having to spend time with this asshole again, but the thought of being the one to finally tell his story, the real deal, which excited me immensely.

It was going to be a story everybody would want to read.

"Good news?" my dad asked with a deep sigh. He was holding my mother's hand. They were still like newlyweds. It was kind of cute, I guess. Gave me hope that it was never too late.

"Yes," I said. "Very good news, indeed. I feel a new book might be coming up soon."

"That's excellent, Emma," my mom said. "Gotta keep writing them, so people don't forget you."

I stared at her. What was that supposed to mean? I had

written so many books in the last couple of years. Was she implying that I wasn't working hard enough? I knew I was behind with the book that was supposed to be published this fall, but there was still time. I worked hard when I needed to.

I shook the thought. This was not the time to start arguing with her. I was way too happy for that. If I landed this story, my editor would be ecstatic. Several journalists over the years had tried to tell the story of Bjarke Lund, the country's biggest psychopath. I mean, with the latest killings, he could go down in the history books as the sickest killer in Danish history. If only I could get him to talk about the other killings that he was acquitted of too. I mean, even if he was cleared of all those killings, I had to assume that he had done those as well, right? I had to assume he stood behind his mother's death, his ex-girlfriend's, and her sons' deaths. I would have to make sure it was mentioned in the contract that he had to talk about all of that as well and be completely honest.

If I succeeded with this, it was going to be big. Like really big.

SIXTY-TWO
AUGUST 2014

"I'm innocent."

The sentence hit me like a blow in the stomach. Was that why he had asked me to come? So he could keep claiming his innocence? I stared at him with an open mouth. I couldn't believe it. I had taken the ferry to the mainland to visit the guy in prison because he had promised me his story, and this was the first thing he said to me when I sat down across from him?

"I'm sorry, what?"

This wasn't at all what I had expected to hear. He wasn't at all the person I had expected. I had thought he would show just a small portion of humility, but he was still wearing that confident and condescending look in his eyes. Like the fact that I was a woman made me somehow automatically inferior to him. It pissed me off, to put it mildly. His entire attitude made me resent him even more.

"I was framed," he continued.

Oh my. He continues!

I leaned in over the table between us. "Listen, buddy. I was promised your story. I'm not writing a book about a guy claiming he's innocent, 'cause the prisons are filled with them. I thought you were ready to tell the truth... the honest truth."

Steffen Carlsen slammed his handcuffed fists onto the table. "Dammit! Why won't anyone ever listen?"

I exhaled. "Come on! You're claiming you were framed? How do you explain the picture of one of the victims in your living room? How do you explain the fact that I saw you there on the night you killed that couple in Sønderho? How do you explain the hair the police found? The ruby red slippers, the DVD case next to your TV. I mean, you painted your face green like the Wicked Witch of the West during an interview, for Christ's sake. You're obviously obsessed with *The Wizard of Oz*. You like to dress the dead women in the ruby red slippers, for some strange sick reason. The way I see it, there really is no way anyone will believe your innocence."

Steffen Carlsen's smile had disappeared. His eyes were flickering. He was slowly realizing the seriousness of the situation. "But I am! I am innocent. I didn't kill any of these people. I need you to help me prove it. No one will believe me. Not even my own attorney."

My blood was boiling. I couldn't believe the nerve that this guy had. Did he really think I was that stupid?

"Well, maybe that's because you have the words guilty written all over your face. Everything points to you. Even the drawing made by the one victim who survived. There really isn't much anyone can do for you anymore. It's over. Finished. You're done."

Steffen Carlsen looked intensely into my eyes. He looked scared. I saw deep fear in them. "I can't go back to prison again. I just can't. It's just like the other times. People want me convicted, and there's nothing I can do about it. I swear to you, Emma, I didn't kill anyone. I never killed anyone. I might have been a bastard for most of my time on this earth, but I could never take someone's life. I swear on everything dear to me; I could never do such a thing. Never. Can't you see how easy it would be for someone to plant that hair at the scene of crime? I did an interview many years ago, painted as the Wicked Witch; I do love *The Wizard of Oz*, it's one of my all-time favorite films, and I've never tried to hide that. Everyone knows it. Anyone who knows me, knows it. Even people who don't know me. It would be so easy to make it look like it was me who did this. And the girl from my wall? Everyone who has ever been to my house has seen that picture. I bring all my classes inside to look at the wall. To tell them they could have a life as great as mine. That if they believed in the power of their penis, they could conquer as many women as I have."

"But, I saw you," I snapped at him. I couldn't believe how much this guy was annoying me right now. The power of their penis? Who said a thing like that? "I saw you there. You looked at me from the red car. Standing under the streetlamp, I saw your face."

"Did you? Or did you see someone dressed like me? You dressed up when you came to my home the other day. It would be very easy to wear a wig with a ponytail and a leather vest like I usually wear when I'm in public. Wouldn't it?"

I hated to admit it, but he made a fair point. He had worn sunglasses when I saw him in the street, so I had no chance of recognizing the eyes. It could have been a disguise. It could.

Everything inside of me screamed that he was guilty. I had no doubt in my mind. He was just playing me. But, with my heart, it was different. A small seed of doubt had been planted, and I had no idea what to do with it.

SIXTY-THREE

AUGUST 2014

He had to be so angry. He had to be so frustrated, so scared sitting alone in that cell, trying to convince the world that he had been framed, yelling at them that he hadn't killed all those people.

She couldn't stop giggling, thinking about it, and about the plan. She sat in front of the mirror while putting her long brown hair in a ponytail. With a pair of tweezers, the beard was carefully placed on the smooth skin on the chin, beginning to look like a goatee. It felt uncomfortable, and she wondered why anyone would ever decide willingly to have a beard.

"So, how does it feel to be back in prison, huh?" she said to her reflection. "Made any new friends yet?"

She found the leather vest and put it on, then tucked the white shirt into the jeans, so the shape of her breasts wouldn't be seen.

Yes, Louise thought. Now she looked just like the Jesper Melander she had known, who had moved into her flat after his release and raped her night after night. The same Jesper Melander who had told her he owned her from now on. This

was how she got to know him. He could change his name all he
wanted to, but he was still the same to her.

For years, she had been Mrs. Melander. For years, she had
been watching him bring young girls home with him, taking
their pictures, taking them to the basement where he could
spend hours with them, while she was left in her room with
nothing but her jealousy for companionship.

"Bet there aren't any girls where you're at now, huh, baby?
Guess you'll have to settle for me for a little while. Poor baby."

Louise stood in front of the mirror and looked at Jesper
Melander. It was amazing how much she looked like him. Especially after she had started working out. The CrossFit exercises
had given her broader shoulders and a wider chest that she
needed to look like a man. It was all part of it.

Louise grabbed the gas can and matches and headed out the
door. The small red car that Louise's parents had once bought
for her was in one of the barns, hidden under a cover. The
police had told her the house would be searched sometime soon,
and had told her to stay in a hotel, and Louise had played along.
She had thrown the act of her life, being all surprised by what
her husband had been up to when they came to arrest him.

But, on the inside, she had been laughing her head off.
Didn't they know it was all just a part of the plan? Didn't they
know they had been led along all the way? Pulled by the nose?
They had been given the clues they needed to bring him down.
Oh, how well she was playing her cards. It was a magnum opus.

She had told them she thought she knew her husband, that
she had no idea what he had been up to. She had told them,
with tears in her eyes, that she had been such an idiot for
marrying him when everyone told her he was scum... that she
was so glad they had figured it out and taken him in before he
killed her as well. She had told them how he had often beaten
her, and that she was afraid of him. Then she had shown them
her latest bruises from the night in the basement. She told the

officers she would pack a bag and stay in a hotel in downtown Nordby. She had cried and told them she could never set foot in this house again.

* * *

But, in reality, she had just stayed at the house on the farm. She knew it would take days before the forensics department from Copenhagen would come to search the house. And, by then, she would be long gone.

It was all a part of the beautiful plan. But, there was still one thing missing, one mission she needed to do first.

Louise started whistling in the car and continued as she parked it in front of Emma Frost's old house by the beach. She grabbed the gas can, and while pouring the gasoline on her house, she was singing her favorite song from *The Wizard of Oz*.

SIXTY-FOUR
AUGUST 2014

The following night, I couldn't stop thinking about my visit to the prison. I couldn't believe it. Could the guy really be innocent? Had we made a mistake?

Don't be a fool. He's just playing you. He's just good at manipulating people. Don't fall for it, Emma. Don't. He did it. He killed those people in cold blood. It all fits.

I tossed and turned for an hour or so, then looked at my phone. It was almost midnight. I went on Facebook to get my mind on something else. I scrolled through my friend's statuses and read an article that stated it contained ten tips to get in shape fast.

I wasn't interested in doing any of them, so I clicked out of Facebook and put my head on the pillow again. Thoughts flickered through my mind and wouldn't leave me alone.

In the distance, I thought I could hear someone singing, but realized it had to be in my head. It was that song from the film that Sophia and I had sung the other day. I opened my eyes, wondering about the lyrics.

It had been my theory that the killer had taken those same things that they wanted in the film, right? He had taken the brain, the heart, and cut out the nerve from someone. But he hadn't taken a home, had he?

Was that going to be his next move? Did they arrest him before he could finish?

"How do you take a home from someone?" I asked into the darkness.

What if it isn't Steffen Carlsen? What if he is as innocent as he claims to be? Is there someone else out there, right now, getting ready to kill again?

I shook the thought. That was just silly. I closed my eyes and tried to go back to sleep, when suddenly, the door to my room opened.

It was Victor. My heart dropped.

"What's up, buddy? Having another bad dream?"

"I'm not afraid of a witch. I'm not afraid of anything—except a lighted match."

"What's that, buddy?" I asked and went to him. He was shaking all over. It scared me.

My heart started pounding, as he repeated the sentence over and over again, just like the other times.

"Is that another quote from the film?"

Could it be another one? It had to be.

I almost panicked. Somewhere out there, someone was about to get killed, and I had no idea who or where.

"Victor, do you know anything that can help me?" I asked, but he kept repeating the sentence over and over again. That was when I saw it. That was when I saw the big bright light outside of my window.

Oh, my. My house is on fire!

The heat was suddenly unbearable; flames were licking the side of the house. I grabbed Victor in my arms and, for once, he didn't complain that I touched him. He let me carry him through the hall and into Maya's room. I pulled her arm. "Maya, baby. Wake up. The house is on fire!"

"What?"

"We need to get out now. Run!"

We jumped the stairs, two at a time, and stomped outside, where we threw ourselves onto the grass, coughing and panting. My kids were both screaming, and so was I at the sight of my wonderful house surrounded by flames. Windows were popping, and curtains took the fire inside. I couldn't believe this. It was like a horrible nightmare.

I heard a voice come up behind me. "Step aside!"

I turned and saw Jack run into the front garden, dragging a huge hose, much like the ones the firefighters used. He turned it on, and water splashed onto the house and soon extinguished the fire. My heart was beating fast, as I held my children close, and the fire slowly died out. My only question was, who the hell had done this?

Little did I know, I was seconds from getting my answer.

SIXTY-FIVE

AUGUST 2014

I heard turmoil and turned my head to see two people on the street outside the neighbor's house, fighting, yelling, and screaming. I let go of my children and ran to see. I was quite startled by the sight that met me.

It was Steffen Carlsen's wife and... and Dr. Sonnichsen? What the heck was this? Why was Louise Carlsen wearing a beard?

Dr. Sonnichsen was on top of Louise Carlsen now, sitting on her, holding her down. "Doctor Sonnichsen?" I asked and approached them.

She was groaning and panting. "She is a fighter, a typical seven. I saw her. She was pouring gasoline on your house and setting it on fire. I had to stop her."

I couldn't believe any of what was happening. Louise Carlsen had set my house on fire? Why?

"I don't understand..." I said.

"She was trying to kill you and your family," Dr. Sonnichsen said, sounding annoyed that I didn't understand.

"But... but why?" I asked.

"Maybe we could ask her that later, like after she's incarcerated?" Dr. Sonnichsen said and fought to keep the woman beneath her down.

"I'm sorry. I'll call the police right away." I fumbled with my phone, then found Morten's number and called it.

"I'm sorry, Morten. I really need your help."

"What's up?" he said.

"I... I don't know where to begin. Maybe you should come down here. Someone tried to set my house on fire."

"I'll be right there."

When Morten said that, he meant it. A few minutes later, he was standing in my front garden, putting Louise Carlsen in handcuffs. The woman kept screaming and laughing like a madman. She had definitely lost it.

Morten put her in his van and drove off. I thanked Dr. Sonnichsen and gave her a warm hug.

"I'm so glad you were here to catch that woman," I said. "How can I ever repay you?"

Dr. Sonnichsen smiled and bowed her head. "It's no big deal."

"What were you doing out here anyway?" I asked.

"I... well, I was just in the neighborhood. I know some very nice people not far from here, and was on my way home, when I saw this person lurking around the house with a can of gas. It looked very suspicious, and when she lit a match, I jumped out of the car and threw myself at her, trying to prevent her from setting the house on fire, but the match fell to the ground just as I did and lit up the house anyway. I couldn't stop it from spreading. I'm sorry about the damage to your house."

"It could have been much worse," I said. "Thanks to you, it wasn't."

"I'll get going then," Dr. Sonnichsen said, and waved to Maya. "See you tomorrow."

Maya waved back, and I watched as the hero of the day walked to her car and drove off.

Sophia, who had also come out of her house once she heard all the noise, came over and hugged me.

"My beautiful house," I said, shedding a tear.

"You can all sleep at my place tonight," she said. "You can stay there as long as you want."

Jack came to me and hugged me too. "Thank you so much," I said. "Without you, my entire house would be burnt to the ground."

"Y-y-you're welcome. We don't have a f-f-fire station on the island, so, many years ago, I v-v-volunteered as a firefighter in case of emergency. Guess today was one of those, huh? It doesn't look too bad, though. M-m- mostly façade work. Maybe the kitchen will need a little r-r-redecorating and your room upstairs, but that should be all. The rest of the house l-l-looks intact."

"Thank you. You have no idea how grateful I am." I kissed his cheek and our eyes met. I smiled, then turned my head and met Sophia's eyes. She was staring at us, looking like she was frozen. I saw something in her eyes I hadn't seen before, and suddenly it struck me. I stared at Jack, then back at her.

"Are you...?"

Sophia nodded and so did Jack.

"It happened a couple of weeks ago. We didn't want to tell you until we knew if it was going somewhere, but I guess it is," Sophia said, walking to him. He put his arm around her shoulders.

I was startled, completely taken aback. But at the same time, I was so incredibly happy for them both.

"You both," I said, with tears in my eyes. "I can't believe it. That is such wonderful news! And Sophia. I can't believe you managed to keep it from me for this long."

Sophia shrugged, while I hugged them both. Guess it was time to let go of the men in my life. Maybe it was about time.

SIXTY-SIX

AUGUST 2014

We moved into a hotel downtown while they worked on my house. I had made the decision to have my entire kitchen redone, even though the damage from the fire didn't require it. I wanted a new kitchen and had thought about it for a long time. It was, after all, the room of the house I spent the most time in. It was my favorite place to be, so it should be nice. It should be up-to-date and have the newest appliances.

The hotel was nice, and the kids and I enjoyed staying there, pretending to be on holiday.

My parents had told us we could come live with them any time we wanted, but I really needed some time alone with my kids and didn't want to have to argue with my mom about all kinds of strange little things like we always did.

Every day, I felt so grateful for still having my life and for nothing horrible happening to my children. I couldn't believe how close it had been.

After a week in the hotel, Morten called me one morning while the kids were in school. I hadn't heard from him since the night of the fire, so it was quite surprising to hear his voice.

"I thought you'd like to know that we have interrogated

Louise Carlsen, and she has admitted to committing all the killings, dressed like her husband."

"Excuse me, what?" I asked, almost choking on the soda I had just grabbed from the minibar. I couldn't believe what he was telling me. Was she the one? I guess it made sense, when you thought about it. She was very strong.

"But how? Why?"

"Apparently, she wanted to frame him because he was constantly cheating on her, bringing home new women all the time. He was into bondage and stuff like that, and they had a basement filled with equipment that he used to torture her, against her will, she told us. She had no idea how to get rid of him or to revenge herself for all the hurt he had brought upon her, so she came up with the kills. She made the shoes herself, to make sure the police would know it was someone who loved the film, like Steffen Carlsen, or whatever his name is now. She took one of his hairs and planted it on the bed next to Camilla Hermansen. We found everything when we searched the house, the craft table to make the slippers, the glitter, and the red spray tins. She was dressed like him in a leather vest and a glued-on beard when we arrested her, and we found more clothes like them in the house where she told us they would be, some of them with blood on them. We even found the knife in her wardrobe behind her clothes. I think it's going to be very easy to convict her fast and put her away."

"Wow!" I was completely blown away. I guess I should have known when I saw her strange outfit and beard while she was fighting with Dr. Sonnichsen. But it all happened so fast, and she was a mess, and her hair was all over the place. Now, it all made sense, I thought. I couldn't believe the guy was actually innocent like he had told me. I guess I owed him an apology.

Not really. He's still a prick, a genuine bastard.

"I know. It's quite the story," Morten said. "But, luckily, we got to the bottom of it, and like I told you, she admitted to doing it all by herself, with the intent of framing her husband. We found the remains of what we believe might be her parents in a freezer in the basement. And get a load of this. We found the heart, the brain, and the nerve in the freezer as well. Plus, she had just started at Realinvest, the island's only realty company six months ago as a real estate agent. It gave her the access she needed to the victims. Plus, she had a very good reason for wanting to get rid of Camilla Hermansen, because she knew she was one of the women sleeping with her husband. Now, I think it's fair to say, it's all over. Case is closed."

"I'm so glad to hear that," I said. "You must be thrilled. Finally, your life can get back to normal."

"Well, it's not going to be normal..." he paused. "At least not without you in it."

My heart was about to melt. I missed him so incredibly much. "Well..." I had no idea what to say. I held the phone tightly to my ear when there was a knock on my hotel room door. "Hold on, there's someone at the door. Wait a second; don't go anywhere. I'll get rid of them. It might be room service. I ordered some lunch."

I put the phone on the table and walked to open the door, wondering why they had brought my lunch at ten-thirty in the morning.

I couldn't believe what I saw standing on the other side of the door. It was Steffen Carlsen.

SIXTY-SEVEN
AUGUST 2014

"What the hell do you want?" I asked.

He looked even more obnoxious than the last time I saw him. Had he come to gloat? To tell me I should have believed him. To have me say that I was sorry. That I was wrong. What?

He didn't ask if he could be let in, but pushed me aside and shoved his way in.

"Hey!" I yelled after him. "You can't just barge in here!"

Steffen Carlsen smacked his hands together with a laugh. The door closed shut behind me.

"I'm here to thank you," he said.

"Thank me for what?"

"For making it all so easy for me. For falling for every trick in the book, for being such a fool. Basically, thank you for being YOU!" he pointed his finger at me and laughed again.

"What do you mean?"

"Ha! You have no idea, do you? You women are so predictable. BOY, it's almost too easy."

His eyes were flickering, and I wondered if he had completely lost it.

He made me feel very uncomfortable.

"You still haven't told me why you're here," I said.

"Ah!" Steffen Carlsen covered his mouth with both hands, and then he moved them and spoke. "It's almost too EXCITING! See, the plan failed on one account. You were supposed to be dead. You were supposed to be the next victim, the home, and the police were going to find the ruby red slippers in the ashes, and then they would know they had the wrong guy. But, that's not how it went. Not that I'm disappointed. No, this way is so much BETTER!"

"Plan? What plan?" I asked, while the pieces of my puzzle started to fall into place. "You planned this with her, didn't you?"

Steffen Carlsen laughed again. "Isn't it beautiful? Magnificent. And I'm here to share the entire secret with you, Emma, only you. I want to see the look in your eyes when I tell you how I can get women to do anything for me. And I do mean ANYTHING!"

"Like, go to prison for you?" I asked.

"YES! Exactly."

"So, someone took the fall for you, and admitted to having killed your ex-girlfriend and her sons? You convinced her to take the fall?"

"She suggested it on her own. She had been writing letters to me during the trial. She told me she would die for me, that's how much she loved me. I told her she could do something almost as good. From there on, it was easy. I just told her where the bodies were buried, and where the bloody axe was that I used to kill them, then she could tell the police, and they would believe it was her. I let her in on every little detail, so they wouldn't see through it, and she told them she was jealous of my ex because she was in love with me. We went over it again and again when she came to visit. I think, in the end, she actually thought she had done it. She lived the act, so to speak. Isn't it wonderful?"

"And, so Louise, your wife, did the same?"

"That woman loves me more than anyone. See, I found out what she really likes." Steffen Carlsen approached me and pushed me up against the wall. It hurt my back and I had the air knocked out of me.

"See, she liked it hard. She liked the pain. And I loved watching her in pain. Just like I like watching you in pain right now," he said, and grabbed me around my throat. I spurted and gasped for air.

"Please... let... me... go."

"Tsk. You're not listening, Emma. You need to listen, or you'll ruin everything. I'm finally spilling the beans here, Emma. I'm telling you everything, just like you wanted me to. I'm telling you I did kill my mother on that night when we were watching *The Wizard of Oz*. I stabbed her with a kitchen knife again and again, while Dorothy followed the yellow brick road. I was so SICK of her and her many different men. You know what they did to me, Emma? They did awful things to me, things you can't even imagine and put in your little books. And my mother watched. She never stopped them. So, once when we had gotten a new home and moved for the thirteenth time and we were sitting in the living room watching my favorite film, she told me she had met someone new, and that he would move in soon. She was so excited. She told me she was in love and promised me that this time it would be different. This one was a good guy. Do you know how many times I'd heard her say that? No, you don't, Emma. You don't know what it's like to be chased around the house, your own home, where you should feel safe as a child, by some man who would beat the crap out of you if he got ahold of you. So, I hacked her into bits and pieces with my axe, while they sang about how they were off to see the wizard. You know that song, Emma. Oh, the wonderful wizard, Emma. You know him, don't you? He's truly wonderful. But the best part is still the witch. I loved the witch, and I still cheer for her to be able to stop them, Emma. But she never does. She never stops them from getting to the wizard. And then she melts. I hate that scene when she melts, and, oh, how I loathe the scream."

Steffen Carlsen loosened his grip on my throat a little. He looked like he was remembering something. "You know what I did when I was done hacking my mother into pieces?"

I shook my head the best I could while gasping for air.

"I rewound the film and watched it all over again. I was sitting there in our new living room, with blood smeared all over me, and I watched the film over and over again, singing along to all the songs. Then, I fed her to the pigs on a nearby farm. I rode there on my bike in the middle of the night with my chopped-up mother in a rubbish bag. They ate everything, and I enjoyed listening to the sound of her bones crunching. I was accused of killing her, but no one could ever prove it. There was no body. They never found her. Now, how did I get Louise to be in on this? Well, it wasn't as hard as you'd think, my dear. First, I helped her kill her parents. I told her what to do and when to do it. She needed to be delivered from them. They were only holding her back. She did it while I was in prison. It was beautiful. I told her about anger and how she should let it grow... that it was her friend. 'Feed the hurt, nourish the pain till it's strong enough to avenge you,' I said. 'Save it inside of you. Treasure it.' And she did it. She stabbed them to death in her own flat, just because I told her to. It was magnificent. She stuffed them inside that freezer and took them with her everywhere we moved. I made her what she is. I created her."

Steffen Carlsen looked me in the eye. He was tightening his grip on my throat. "They would jump to their death for me, Emma. Do you understand that? Do you understand what kind of power that leaves me with?"

I tried to nod, but he was holding me too hard, choking me. I was begging for my life now.

"Please..." I pleaded.

"No, Emma, dear. You know how all things must come to an end. Even good and fun things. This is your curtain call, Emma. Now that you know everything, you must die."

His gloved hands were pressing harder now, and I could no longer breathe. I saw light flicker before my eyes and an overwhelming dizziness came over me. In my dying moments, all I could think of was my children. Who was going to take care of them? Michael?

In the distance, in my suffering darkness I heard a well-known song whispered in my ear. A lullaby about a rainbow.

SIXTY-EIGHT

AUGUST 2014

I never knew how it happened. All I know is that I was floating in a sea of stars above the rainbow, when suddenly, I was drastically pulled out of my dream. It felt like a tornado pulling my legs, dragging me back to harsh reality.

I woke up to the sound of people fighting, and when I opened my eyes, I saw Morten and Steffen Carlsen going at each other.

I coughed and tried to breathe, but my throat hurt so badly, I threw up on the carpet.

Steffen Carlsen threw a punch at Morten and forced him to fly backward, hitting the table behind him with a loud scream.

"Morten!" I yelled, and tried to get up, but the dizziness kept me down. Steffen Carlsen was up fast and threw himself at Morten, punching him hard. I had just enough air to scream.

"Morten!"

Blood spurted onto the wall. I screamed again and covered my eyes. Finally, I got to my feet, while Steffen Carlsen kept punching Morten. I tried to walk but fell flat to the ground again.

Steffen Carlsen was above Morten again. Morten lay lifeless on the ground, while receiving more punches and kicks to the stomach. I was terrified. As I fell flat to the ground, I spotted Morten's gun. Steffen Carlsen must have somehow managed to get it from him, and he must have dropped it in the fight. It didn't matter how it got there, but it mattered that I could reach over and pick it up in my shaking hands.

I tried hard to get it to stay still in my hands when I pointed it toward Steffen Carlsen.

He laughed when he saw me. Then danced around while chanting, quoting the Cowardly Lion. Then, he jumped toward me, and as he landed on top of me, I did the only thing I could at that moment. I pulled the trigger and shot him in the stomach.

Then, I threw the gun and ran to Morten. I lifted his head and held it between my hands. "Oh, my. Please tell me you're all right. Please, Morten. I'll never leave you again. I promise. We'll figure it out, Morten." I hugged his bloody face, as I heard noises in the hallway. Soon, the room was filled with people.

"Call for help!" I screamed. "Call for help!"

"Did you mean it?"

I looked down. Morten's gentle eyes were looking back at me.

"Morten!"

"So, did you?" he asked again through the pain.

"Lie still till help comes. Did I what?"

"Did you mean what you said before? That you would never leave me again?"

I swallowed a lump of tears, and then smiled. I stroked his cheek. "Yes. We'll figure it out, won't we?"

He smiled and closed his eyes as more people rushed in. One of them told me he was a doctor on holiday. He could help, he said. Half an hour later, Morten was picked up by a helicopter and taken to the hospital in Esbjerg.

EPILOGUE

"One, two, skip a few... ninety-nine, one hundred."

The numerologist skipped along the sidewalk. She was in an incredibly good mood this morning. She was doing so well. She was getting very close to the family now, and they still didn't suspect a thing. No, they didn't. And that thing, the incident... the fire had been like it was sent from heaven. She couldn't have planned it better herself. Again, it had been the numbers making sure she was there at the right moment. At one minute to midnight. *One again.*

Best of all, was that Emma Frost hadn't suspected a thing. Apparently, she believed her little story about being outside of her house coincidentally. Didn't she know that nothing was coincidental? Nothing at all. It was all written in the numbers and the stars.

She had been outside of Emma Frost's house because she was keeping an eye on her and her family, monitoring every moment of her life. She still did that. While tutoring Maya Frost, the numerologist had put up small cameras in Emma Frost's home, and that way she could see everything they were up to, every little movement. Even when she was having sex with that awful boyfriend of hers, who was now back from the hospital and was staying at her house while Emma took care of him.

Apparently, they were back together again... having sex all the time, being all over each other. It complicated things slightly, but it wasn't something the numerologist couldn't handle.

She would still go on with her plan... her plan to get rid of Emma Frost. She wanted it done properly. That was the real reason why she had stopped that crazy woman from burning down the house. It wasn't supposed to happen like that. Emma Frost's death should be spectacular. And it certainly shouldn't be left in the hands of someone as incompetent as that woman.

Instead, it had come as an opportunity for the numerologist to win the trust of Emma Frost. All she needed was to get just close enough to make her move. Emma Frost was never going to know what hit her. Never. All she was waiting for now was the right time and place. The numbers would tell her. They never let her down. It was all written in the numbers.

A LETTER FROM WILLOW

Dear Reader,

I want to say a huge thank you for choosing to read *There's No Place Like Home*. If you enjoyed it and want to keep up to date with all my latest releases, just sign up at the following link. Your email address will never be shared, and you can unsubscribe at any time.

www.bookouture.com/willow-rose

I hope you loved *There's No Place Like Home* and if you did, I would be very grateful if you could write a review. I'd love to hear what you think, and it makes such a difference helping new readers to discover one of my books for the first time.

As always, I want to thank you for all your support and for reading my books. I love hearing from my readers—you can get in touch through social media or my website, or email me at madamewillowrose@gmail.com.

Take care,

Willow

KEEP IN TOUCH WITH WILLOW

www.willow-rose.net

f facebook.com/willowredrose

X x.com/madamwillowrose

instagram.com/willowroseauthor

BB bookbub.com/authors/willow-rose

PUBLISHING TEAM

Turning a manuscript into a book requires the efforts of many people. The publishing team at Bookouture would like to acknowledge everyone who contributed to this publication.

Commercial
Lauren Morrissette
Hannah Richmond
Imogen Allport

Cover design
The Brewster Project

Data and analysis
Mark Alder
Mohamed Bussuri

Editorial
Jennifer Hunt
Sinead O'Connor

Proofreader
Joni Wilson

Milton Keynes UK
Ingram Content Group UK Ltd.
UKHW010728110724
445512UK00004B/69

9 781835 253359